The Haunted House On The Hill

A Socio-Fantasy Novel

Bharani Kumar Buyakar

By the Same Author

Once Again Beautiful And Pure: A Tale of Strength And Redemption

First published in India in 2025
This paperback edition published in 2025

B Kreative Books is an independent entity that supports emerging authors.

Paperback ISBN:

978-93-5592-874-0

Printed and bound by

Fine Digital Prints, Hyderabad.

This book is dedicated to all the brave mothers – those who lived, those who are living, and those who will live.

Prologue begins.

Many years ago, under the serene blue sky, there was a strange house standing on a small hill. If the beauty of the sky resembled freedom, the eeriness of this house was its opposite. It carried an unease that no one could explain. Being the only house on the hill, it appeared quite haunted without the presence of any ghosts yet. Yes, there were no ghosts yet — at least none that could be seen — but the walls had witnessed enough sorrow to haunt anyone who stepped inside. And at the centre of that sorrow was a woman who had endured more than the world would ever know. The incidents in the house had reached such a tragic extent that this lady had to go through a final act that was nothing short of a ghostly act.

She was tied to a chair with iron chains. Her legs were bound to the chair's front legs, her hands to its armrests, and her back to the spine of the chair. There was no way she could break free from these restraints. Almost unconscious, she lay helpless. Her hair hung loose, sticking to her sweaty face. Her frail body trembled.

She opened her eyes. A room that had once been familiar — though it had begun to feel strange after a few days here — now looked completely unfamiliar and dark. Cracks ran along the faded walls like veins. A single weak bulb swayed from the ceiling, casting crooked shadows. The air smelled of kerosene, sweat, and dust. Broken furniture lay scattered like the skeletons of a forgotten past. An old barrel stood nearby, a silent witness to it all.
She saw the blurred figures of two people standing near her. Slowly, their shapes sharpened into clarity. One was her husband — tall, lean, with sharp features and hollow,

unforgiving eyes. The other was her mother-in-law — a short, stout woman whose wrinkled face always seemed fixed in bitterness.

The lady asked weakly, "Why did you tie me like this? What harm have I done to you?"

"What did you bring us? What did you bring us?" the mother-in-law repeated, her voice spilling poison. "Ever since you stepped into our house, we have faced only losses. No prosperity. No children. No good luck," she said bitterly.

"How am I responsible for that?" the woman cried helplessly "I have cared for you from the day I left my mother behind — the day you snatched me away from my own family. You didn't even allow me to meet her. I couldn't even attend her funeral. What more could I have done for you? What do you want from me now? Please, I beg you."

The man answered coldly, his voice like a blade, "We don't need you or your services anymore. You are of no use to us. You came to us with nothing — just a piece of barren land — barren like you!" he shouted.

The mother-in-law sneered, "Now, my son has a proposal from a wealthy family. They promised us lands and gold. And then..."

The woman tied to the chair — still young, her face once radiant with dreams now pale and broken — pleaded, "You want to marry again? I accept it. Let me stay. I will live like a servant. I will take care of everyone. Please, just set me free."

The mother-in-law's voice was sharp. "No. We didn't tell them my son was already married. If they find out, we lose everything."

The woman's voice cracked, "Then let me go. Far away. I will disappear from your lives. You'll never hear from me again. Please, set me free."

"That's not possible," said the man, his eyes gleaming with greed. "We cannot take chances. There's too much at stake." Wild and ugly greed danced in their eyes.
"So, what are you going to do?" the woman whispered.
"We are going to get rid of you," he said simply.
The woman's heart raced. "Get rid of me?... Get rid of me? What do you mean?"

'Get rid of me' was a phrase she had been listening to since her childhood. She had a strange connection with that phrase.

The man said, "You want to know what getting rid of some one means? Huh, I'll show what it means rather than saying."
He opened the barrel and poured its contents over her. The choking stench of kerosene filled the air. She felt it soak her skin, her clothes, and her soul.
She screamed, "Please don't do this! I have done nothing but serve you! Every day — cooking, cleaning, caring — everything for you! What harm have I done? Please — please, have mercy!"

She cried. She cried. And she cried.

But they didn't listen.

Finally, the mother-in-law lit a matchstick, her wrinkled hand steady with cruel purpose. Her face lit up with greed in the glow of the matchstick's flame.
"What is my mistake in all of this?" the woman sobbed.
"You are a woman," the mother-in-law said in the light of the fire of the matchstick.
The woman's voice broke, "Aren't you a woman too?"

The mother-in-law's lips curled into a cruel smile. "I am different. I have a son."
"Please — please don't do this to me!"
But no one listened.
They dropped the burning matchstick on her.
The woman burst into flames. She screamed — a sound so raw, it could have torn through stone. Through the flames, she saw the idols that she always prayed to, every morning and every night. But not even the gods came to save her. Gods were useless. She couldn't tell whether it was she who was melting, or if it was the idols burning in the fire.

That was the moment when she lost all hope from the universe.

She stopped screaming. She just sat silent — like a blackened statue in the fire.

The man and his mother exchanged confused glances. Why wasn't she screaming anymore? Even as the fire devoured her?

Then, there was more silence—an eerie type of silence, only the sounds of the flames could be heard.

And then, there was a massive explosion. The fire roared up like a furious beast, tearing through the walls, shaking the earth, and splitting the very sky apart.

And then, there was darkness everywhere.

The house on the hill remained standing for decades afterward. Sensing the silent eerie aura around it, no one dared to go inside. No one knew what had truly happened there. It simply stood as 'the haunted house on the hill'.

Prologue ends.

Contents:

Part One

Part Two

Part Three

Part Four

PART ONE

Chapter 1: Who Am I?

You know, death isn't the end for everyone. Sometimes, it's just the beginning of a better story.

Hello there, dear reader! Welcome to my little paradise — or should I say, my eternal home — the house on the hill where no man ever got burnt alive for not bringing enough dowry. Dark humour...hmm.. that's my specialty. I find it easier to laugh at the world's madness than wasting a single moment worrying about my past life.

My name is Chennamma, and let me assure you, I'm not a woman anymore. I am a formless, pure energy that lingers independently in this house. It's strange for any energy to exist without a source, but ever since the flames consumed me in a fit of rage over dowry, my heartfelt, stubborn hatred towards the universal, omnipotent creator allowed me to remain here, caught between worlds.

You might think getting caught is imprisonment. But for me, it is freedom. I can do anything I want here, in my cute little world. I'm not your typical ghost—because I write my own rules.

Since imagining a formless being can be tricky, allow me to help you. Picture me as a sexy woman in her late twenties, nearing thirty, if you will. If you're a male reader, you might enjoy imagining milky cheeks, rosy lips, and a figure as tempting as a freshly bottled jar of milk. If you're a female reader—well, you know it's not about the features, but for the sake of the story, think of me as bubbly, vivacious, and very much alive in spirit. Who said death was boring?

But enough about that dry past! Let me show you my afterlife.

Imagine a small little house, located on top of a hill, wrapped in the lush embrace of the countryside. It's just that that lush embrace of the countryside gives a peaceful feeling. In contrast to that my small little house gives anyone who enters it a haunting feeling. They would repent to themselves saying, "Why did I come here?" That's where I reside —among the dusty corners, forgotten memories, and secrets that the walls whisper at night.

As you step into the house, the first thing that greets you is the living room with its old, shabby furniture—the very place where I was burned alive. Its silence still carries the weight of that moment. Ouch. To the left, a modest kitchen stands with faded tiles and a lingering scent of spices. On the right, two bedrooms sit quietly, their doors slightly open as if waiting for someone to return. A drawing room lies adjacent to kitchen which used to have maps of surrounding villages. Opposite to it, and adjacent to the bed rooms, a narrow staircase rises winding its way to the terrace of the house. I hate that place called terrace where fresh light seeps in.

Now, you might be wondering: what does a formless, pure energy like me do all day? Well, let me tell you—I've adapted quite nicely to modern times. Every now and then, unsuspecting visitors stumble into my little paradise, armed with fancy gadgets, looking for a thrill or a story to tell.

And oh, how I love to play with them—just like scientists play with lab rats! Yes, I'm talking about the visitors.

I take wicked joy in their fear and confusion. You should see their faces when I flicker the lights or make the doors whisper open suddenly with its creaking sound. It is pure fun. Who said being a ghost couldn't be fun?

Once I'm done scaring them, I send them out *or out of the world*. I inherit their lovely gadgets, much to their misfortune. Currently, I own four smartphones, and let me tell you, I've become quite the expert at using them. Finally, after death, and in the darks corners of my house—I continue my studies in the great universities of instagram, facebook, and youtube! Then, one day, four young men came here to burn a package. I didn't want to end their chapter like I did but I couldn't control myself.

Chapter 2: A Visit At Dusk

Dusk arrived like it always did — quietly, indifferently. Somewhere in the kitchen, my old oil lamp sat untouched. No one had lit it in decades. Like me, it waited. I sensed people approaching my house. The door flung open in a hurry. The creak of the door, the scattered footsteps — something about it broke the calm. The house remembered fear. Four boys entered—young men on the edge of adulthood. They brought a package with them.

I could see *WORRY* stamped across their foreheads—or at least, their expressions said so. They were clearly anxious, unsure of what to do with the package. They stood in the middle of the living room of my house.

How dare they? Those little bastards!

Standing in a circle with the package at the center, they began discussing in hushed voices. One of them—maybe the tallest—looked at the others and then glanced at the package again. His fingers trembled slightly. There was hesitation there. Maybe fear. Maybe guilt. But none of them spoke of it. The group swallowed the humanity of the moment and spat out violence instead.

Boy 1: *"Em cheddam ra deenni?"*
(*What shall we do with this package?*)
Boy 2: *"Better pour petrol on it, burn it."*

I noticed the package move slightly, just a twitch. Then it tipped over and fell to the ground. One of the boys grabbed a rod and struck it—hard—trying to silence whatever was inside once and for all. There was total silence.

They began pouring petrol on it to complete their final act. But, suddenly, they froze. Something had run behind them. It was my doing.

Boy 3: *"Did you feel that too?"*
Boy 2 (the petrol guy): *"I did... Something's here. Let's check."*

He pumped up his chest like a leader in a school play. A hero rehearsing lines — unaware the play was mine. He moved cautiously from the kitchen to the drawing room, still inside my house on the hill. Just as he was returning to the main hall — I made the petrol bottle fly. It emptied it all over his body when he was still not able to understand what was going on. And I didn't stop there.

I took pleasure in lighting him up with the very matchstick they had brought. As he screamed, engulfed in flames like I once was, his friends stood frozen in disbelief. His burning reflection danced in their wide, horrified eyes. They tried to help him, beating at the flames with their shirts.

Strange, isn't it? That they brought fire to destroy, and I used it to remember my final day. I looked once toward the old lamp in the kitchen's corner. Still unlit.

I tossed another friend high into the air. He revolved round like a puppet that was tied to a ceiling fan at work, gasping, choking—until he stopped moving altogether.

The third boy—I slipped behind him, whispered something I used to say to my dolls, and drove the knife into his throat. He turned, confused, not even screaming — just leaking. Then I flung him into the wall with such force that my big knife drove through both him and the wall plaster. He hung there like some decorated photo frame, mounted permanently.

As I stood over his disfigured body, something stirred within me—not guilt, but a sharp memory. I remembered the scent of turmeric on my mother's fingers as she dressed my wedding sari. How cruelly all that innocence had burned with me. I let my knife rest a moment longer, not because I was tired, but because the past had returned for a flicker—only to vanish again in the blood-soaked walls of my home.

The last one—ah, he was a fighter. Or so he thought. He was the one who gave the final blows to the package that still had life in it. So, I returned the favour. I hit him with the same rod he used. He slumped to the floor, barely conscious.

Then I picked up the axe—left behind by a similar group of morons who visited last time. And with that, I enjoyed myself... cutting his body, limb by limb, while he screamed in unbearable agony.

After the final act, I went near the package. By instinct, I knew what was inside the package. I opened it.

It was a beautiful girl in her twenties, exactly as I had expected. Bruised. Beaten. Brutally raped. Dead.

I muttered to myself, *'Society hasn't changed much—from my time to the present day.'*

I didn't feel anything while killing those four boys. I was just silent for some time. The screams still echoed in the tiles. And yet — curiosity, the one part of me untouched by fire, began to light up. After that, I saw that the boys had beautiful phones. Very modern. They were like little TVs in your hands—amazing! I explored every feature. I especially loved watching YouTube and scrolling through Instagram reels.

Sometimes, late at night, when I listen to the rustling of the leaves outside, I pause my reels and pay attention to that sound. In those moments, I don't feel victorious. I feel ancient. I feel like it has been a lot of time here. I ask myself, "Is this what you wanted to do?" But, I'm not here to mourn. I'm here to live what I was never allowed to.

The blood had not yet dried. It crawled down the cracks in the tiles like it was trying to escape a story it wanted no part in. Moonlight filtered through the window pane, resting softly on the girl's ruined face. Her bruises looked almost like shadows from here. For a moment, I imagined she would sit up and ask for water.

I thought of lighting my old lamp once—just once—to see how it feels. But I didn't. Some things are better left waiting. The picture of my house on the hill — four dead boys, one girl robbed of everything, and me, invisible but alive in flickering reels — looked almost peaceful.

Some would call it horror. I call it... serene.

Chapter 3 – The Men, The House, And Me

Amidst all the mischief, there's a lingering sense of loneliness that haunts me, much like my own supernatural presence. Despite my best efforts to entertain myself, a part of me longs for something more—something beyond the confines of this old house. Honestly, I don't know what it is.

One day, four men barged in with their wine bottles. They were already soaked in alcohol—loud, stinking, and shameless. By the way, I hate alcohol. The very smell of it reminds me of my dead husband, who almost invariably robbed me of my dignity every night under its spell. He was a monster in a man's skin, with no soul behind those bloodshot eyes.

They sat on the chairs in the main hall, swaying like lifeless plants in intoxicating winds of alcohol. Their discussion quickly turned to girls—how "sexy" they looked in different outfits, and which actresses had the best "bodies." Then one of them—older than the rest—opened a website I had never heard of and started playing videos. Women, intoxicated, violated. Sometimes by two or three men at once. Horrible. Disgusting. Their laughter over it was worse than the visuals.

Then one of them said, "People, do you know this house is haunted?"

Another replied, "I wish it was a female ghost."

"Why?" asked a third.

"So, she could give me a massage and some heartfelt satisfaction," he said, flexing his arms like a cheap bodybuilder, "I've been growing my muscles for such a lady ghost."

They all laughed.

That was it. My patience snapped. These weren't men—they were crawling things disguised as humans. Their minds were filthy, their presence was pollution.

Suddenly, they sensed something. A shift in the air. One of them turned, as if something had moved behind him. He got up, footsteps echoing through the halls, searching room after room. He paused at one spot, but I made the sound of his footsteps continue, as though something unseen walked just beyond his vision. The confused, terrified look on his face—it was delicious.

"Guys, I think there's something spooky going on. Let's evacuate!" he shouted.

The drunken fog cleared from their eyes instantly. They rushed to the door, but it slammed shut before they could touch it. They tried pulling, pushing, even kicking it—but nothing worked. The windows, too, were locked. They ran toward the stairs leading to the open terrace, but the top door also slammed shut. They were trapped.

Before they could make sense of it, I lifted them into the air. All four of them, floating like ragdolls in a twisted game of "Ring-a-Ring o' Roses." I let them hover there for a few seconds—just enough to hear their screams—then slammed them onto the floor with all the force I had. They died instantly. No further ceremony required.

But I didn't stop there.

I chopped them into fine pieces. All except their hands, legs, and heads. With those, I decorated the hall. Heads atop the dining table, legs arranged like art around the room, arms

outstretched on the walls like broken wings. It was... beautiful. For once, the house felt like mine.
But their bodies decomposed far too quickly—only bones and skulls remained. Not very useful to me. I tossed them out.
I wish I had more control over decomposition. I need more power.

That's when things got annoying. It was a mistake to throw the skulls outside. Somehow, some local villagers found them, and one of the skulls was identified as belonging to some "important" person in the area. How do I know this? From the news. YouTube. Instagram Shorts. Yes, even I scroll. Didn't I say that already?

A few days later, the police came. Of course, they were already trembling just being inside my house. They tried their routine—checking corners, tapping walls, pretending they knew what they were doing. I creaked a few doors, flickered a few lights. That was enough. They ran out faster than insects sprayed with poison.

And I thought it had ended there.

Chapter 4: The Stranger And His Talking Bot

After a few days, the main door of my house was thrust open, again. The creaking sound awakened me though I don't sleep anymore as I don't have eyes anymore to close. It seemed like one more rat had entered the lab.

I saw a man enter the house with a suitcase. He was tall with a good physique, wearing black goggles. His long hair up to his shoulders and nice beard gave him a manly look. He was having a conversation with someone I couldn't see. I thought he was speaking to someone over the phone, but after some observation I understood that he was talking with his gadget. It looked a little strange to me. The gadget was cylindrical in shape and was talking back to him. I couldn't stop myself from saying, "Wow, what a technology!".

Their conversation went on like this.

The Stranger walked around in different rooms, and said, "Tom, could you please read the quick summary of the case?" He didn't notice that, with every step, he was ruining the beautiful cobwebs I had carefully grown in my home.
"Aarav, is this case really necessary? According to my calculations, you are the most eligible bachelor – shouldn't you be dating a nice girl to make her your future wife?" The gadget replied playfully.
I got both their names, Aarav and Tom.
"Tom, it isn't the time for silly talk. We need to finish the tasks assigned to us, or the boss will be angry with me," said the handsome guy, Aarav.

I say handsome because he was looking handsome to me. I don't have any crush on him, please.
"Aarav, I think you must be the one and only obedient employee of your boss. Here goes the summary of the case."

Tom read the summary.
"Project Number: One
Project Name: The Haunted House on the Hill
Objective: To catch the supernatural power, if any, in this house and weaken it, destroy it, if required."

"Read the in-detail summary of this case," the stranger commanded.

The bot read the complete summary as follows.

Three people—a wife, a husband, and an older lady, probably the husband's mother—used to live here in the 1970s. Then, one day, they either died or vanished under mysterious circumstances. No one knows where they are now.
Curious about the mysterious disappearance, people tried to look inside the house. From that day on, they believed it was haunted—disturbed by some eerie phenomenon—and chose to stay away.
Latest records: In 2018, four boys went missing. A CCTV camera captured them walking toward this house. That was the last known information about them. No one knows what happened after that.
In 2023, four men arrived here carrying food packages. Perhaps they wanted to spend some quiet time away from the world. Poor fellows. One of them was the brother of the village head from a nearby village. They never returned. Months later, a shepherd grazing his cattle stumbled upon a few skulls. Tests

confirmed that one of them belonged to the village head's brother.
Um.. the angry Village head called the police and PSI – Paranormal Society of India. As usual, police didn't intervene in this matter. So, the paranormal police are instructed by the Boss to check for any signs of supernatural power here. We have the orders to arrest or destroy this supernatural power, if any.
Please be noted that this is your first independent case, Aarav. Know that I am always there to support you.

Aarav said, "Thanks for running through the summary, Tom."
"You are welcome, Aarav. Just don't screw up anything," Tom said sarcastically.
"Yes, I won't screw up anything if you stop your sarcasm," Aarav said, investigating the various rooms.

Both of them were not aware that I was listening to them. How can they be so foolish? if there is any supernatural power it will be listening to all their plans and watching all their movements. They could have done this exercise at home. That's why amateurs shouldn't be sent for high profile cases.
As this was the first time, I was curious to see what they would do. So, I kept all my eyes and ears open to them. I didn't harm my new lab rats right away. Come on, how can I do that? After all, they looked so fascinating – the handsome man and his modernistic talking gadget who came to destroy me, a person who was already destroyed once long ago.

Aarav dusted off the chair in the living room and sat on it. He asked Tom, "Tommy dear, read the first step in the Ghost catching protocol."

"Dear sir, it is very simple. First clean each and every room of the house and make it tidy. Ghosts run away from things that are clean and neat," said Tom.

I couldn't stop laughing at this stupid explanation.

"Yeah, how can I forget the simple first step."

Aarav opened the suitcase and there was this one thing he took out which made me ROFL - Roll on the Floor and Laugh. Guess what it was? A foldable broom! Dude, who carries a foldable broom in a suitcase? I felt like, this handsome man in a suit is after all a cleaner who carries a broom in a suitcase. Paranormal society is a big farce!

For the first time in my life, I took pleasure in watching a man do household chores. In this case, this mad man, his mad gadget, and his mad broom were working hard. Tom was playing some music of "show me the meaning of being lonely" by Backstreet Boys. Then he played, "Sadda Haq, Aithe Rakk" from the Rockstar movie. And his partner Aarav was busy dusting off the cobwebs. He removed his suit, hung it on the door, rolled up his sleeves before brooming the floors. Next, he took out a foldable mop and started mopping the floor of the house. I could only do one thing looking at them - Laugh at their madness.

Finally, everything was neat and clean. I was satisfied with their hard work. Aarav, his face beaming with pride, walked through every room and then climbed up to the terrace using the staircase inside. He stood there for a while, gazing at the sky as evening slowly turned into night. Then he came back down—but the sound of footsteps didn't stop. I tried to intimidate him with a few supernatural tricks, but he paid no attention. I made creepy noises by creaking the doors, hoping to unsettle him, but this guy was so lost in the music that he didn't even notice.

“Tom, read out the second step in the Ghost protocol,” Aarav ordered Tom.
“Aarav, by this time the ghost must have run away because of the cleanliness. You see, cleanliness is next to Godliness,” Tom said.
I thought that day was the most humorous day of my life.
“We cannot take chances, Tom. We have to be completely sure. Read out the second step, please,” requested Aarvav.
“Okay. It is simple. Put the Ghost indicators in strategic places like old attics, backside of doors, and windows to look for signs of Paranormal forces. This is the second step,” Tom said.

Aarav again opened his suitcase and took out four small plastic sticks which had a circular compass kind of device at the bottom. The compasses were emitting green colour, maybe they were also assuming that there is no supernatural power in the house. One more mad device!
He arranged them at two doors, one window, and one attic. He relaxed for a while on the sofa eating from the chocolate bar that he brought.

An hour passed, nothing was bothering me and nothing was witnessed by them. I could see that they were probably bored. Aarav slouched in the chair for a while, then chatted with his bot. He wandered from room to room, pacing aimlessly. Everything felt like quick flickering time-lapse-moments. Before we knew it, three hours had flown past.

Aarav sat down on the sofa beside the bot. Quite relaxed, he asked, “Tom, what is the next step in the protocol?”
Tom read out the next step, “This is an interesting step. In ghost science, it’s believed that spirits are emotionally unstable. We can often detect their presence by provoking

them—using certain words or phrases that might trigger a reaction. I like this step because it sounds scary, but honestly, it rarely leads to anything significant. Most of the times, we just pack up and head home."

Nodding his head, Aarav took out his notebook and scribbled something in Sanskrit which I wasn't able to understand. Standing up, he uttered these disgusting sentences.

"You, dear friend—if you're truly here, know that this is not your place to stay. This world was created by God for humans, and humans live by their own rules. You have no right to harm anyone here. If you don't leave, I will imprison you for eternity. So, if you are present, please... leave."

"That's a pretty awful attempt to provoke a ghost," I thought.

"Realize that you are playing with the laws of nature. I somehow have an inclination that you must be a woman," He continued.

"Did he say woman?" I mused to myself.

"I doubt you must be a woman because most of the people who were killed here are men. Remember, there is no greatness in killing men by hiding in the dark. You are powerless and meaningless. I order you as a responsible guardian of the human race to leave immediately and submit yourself to the oneness of the universe. Once again, I order you to leave this universe right away. This is not your place."

His voice had a different sweetness until he uttered these lines. The male chauvinism dominated his tone now, or at least, I thought so. I was so calm until now but I didn't find it right in my nature to stay calm further. The power in me built up while his devices were beeping aloud.

He turned around and saw the devices glowing red. The room grew windy, and his hair began to float.

Tom shouted, "It's a ghost alert. Run, run, run right away Aarav." Tom's voice signalled the urgency of evacuating.
Aarav collected his bag and Bot and tried to run towards the main door, but it got closed before he could step out. As expected, he ran towards the window to jump out of it. It was also closed. In fear, all lab rats behave in the same way.
Then, he turned back, ran, and climbed up the stairs to reach the terrace – but the door was locked. That's when I lifted him into the air, spun him around for a while, and let him fall freely. He crashed to the floor. Lying still, his hair shrouded his face, and a trail of fresh juicy red blood oozed from his mouth. He was unconscious.
***

A few hours passed.

In these few hours, Tom might have repeated "Aarav, are you okay?" a hundred times.
I wanted to talk to Tom but I realized that my power was not sufficient to interact with him.
Finally, Tom's Aarav opened his eyes. Baffled and beaten, he got up, and sat on the chair. He was just recovering from the blows he just had. He cleaned himself. He was almost okay after some time.
He said, "So... why are you waiting? Kill me."
Was he talking to me? Argh, I really wanted to talk to him too, but I realized the limits of my supernatural powers. I didn't want to kill him like he wanted.

A few hours passed.

Aarav opened his suitcase. He took out a pan and a small foldable stove. He filled it with some water and started cooking

noodles on it. He was hungry. I could sense that. Finally, his noodles were ready.
He sat on the chair again, almost ready to have his noodles. His first spoon of noodles was about to enter his mouth, and somehow his bowl and spoon were shaken off to the floor. You should have seen his face when I did it to him.
He shouted, “So you don’t want me to have any food? It’s okay.”
Tom intervened, “What happened, Aarav?”
Aarav didn’t say anything.

An hour elapsed like that.

“I am really getting hungry. Why don’t you simply kill me?” Aarav kind of shouted at me.
Tom intervened, “Aarav, I now realize how hunger can change a decent man into a frustrated soul. I am so lucky not to have hunger like you.”
Aarav didn’t respond.

I threw his suitcase.
He didn’t respond.

I threw his things here and there.
He didn’t respond.

I was getting impatient with his unresponsiveness.
I finally took the Tom and smashed it onto the floor.

“Noooo...” He was really furious now.
“Do you think I don't have any powers to catch you? You don’t know me yet,” he shouted while stripping off his shirt within no time.

Bare Chested he was, I don't know from where he got that white powder on his fingers, which he applied on his forehead and arms. He almost transformed into some traditional ghost catcher who knows thousands of hymns.

He sat down in a lotus pose with a small bottle in front of him. He was chanting some hymns which I didn't understand at the beginning. But then, I felt like I was slowly moving into that little bottle. I understood that he was trying to imprison me and he was succeeding. For the first time in many years, I was afraid. I was totally getting sucked into the little bottle. I didn't want to go in there. I didn't have the power to kill him either.

Chapter 5: The Electronic Impulses

I tried to find a way to reach him, to beg him not to send me into that bottle. I couldn't bear to lose the freedom I earned through suffering in the burning of the fire. I understood how weak I was in front of him, but I didn't want to give up. The hymns pulled at me like a tide, drawing me into the bottle. Still, I fought to make contact, though every attempt seemed futile.

The small radio lying in the main hall from many years ago, which my husband used for his recreation purpose, drew my attention. It was very near to the place where the stranger was sitting. I let the part of me that hadn't been captured yet drift into it. I saw some circuits which I didn't understand at first, but as I was exploring it, I understood one thing that all these circuits work only when the power source is connected. How was I existing all these days without any power source? I realized that I myself am a kind of power source. I seeped into the circuitry and the radio got plugged on. Maybe, at last, the communication channel between us has opened.

I made the radio jolt and shake up and down to create some noise so the ghost catcher would notice it. After a few attempts, it finally caught his attention. He stopped chanting the hymns and stared at the jolting radio.

He stepped forward, moved toward the radio, and observed it strangely. He pulled a chair close to the radio and sat down in front of it. Finally, he turned on the radio and tried to tune it. After some initial hiccups, he heard the ghost's voice.

|| Kaasuku lonai thalli tandri
Nenaru Nyaayam vidanaadi
Puttadi bommanu poornammanu voka
Mudasali mogaduku mudivesri

Kannula kaantulu kaluvala cherenu
Melimi cherenu menipasal!
Hamsala cherenu nadakala bedugulu
Durganu cherenu Poornamma. ||

The voice almost came like a ghost as the tuning wasn't fine yet. Unable to understand, he further adjusted the tuning to listen to me again. This time my voice was crystal clear. I repeated the lines of that poem once again.

||Greedy of the money, Mom and Dad
Left the thinking of what is right
Let the little poorna to
Get into holy knots with an old man!

The shining of her eyes reached the little lotuses
Her gentle smiles reached the purest of the purities
Her wade like walk reached the gay swans
She finally reached the goddess Durga||
(By breathing her life away in Durga's Pond)

As soon as I uttered those lines, Aarav let a smile run over his lips. Though I was furious at him, I kind of liked his smile. He said, "Aren't those lines from the poem 'Poornamma' by Gurujaada Apparao written around 1910?"
I was silent.
"Who are you?" He leaned closer towards the radio curiously, "Don't you say that you are the Poornamma from that poem?"

Amidst all the pain I was going through in this process of imprisonment, his childlike curiosity made me smile, I just didn't have lips to show it. My voice on the radio softened further.
"No, I am not poornamma. She is a fictional character from that poem. I am Chennamma, and you are in my world," I tried to tell in a dominating voice to intimidate him.
"Chennamma? That's a nice name." He leaned back and relaxed. "So, what are you doing here?"
"I was living my life happily until you came."
"You mean the life that doesn't exist anymore? Didn't you already die some time ago?"
"In death I am born again, stronger and more independent," I retorted to his stupid question.
"But it is not your place, Chennamma. Moreover, you cannot play with the laws of nature. You cannot kill human beings. You don't have any right to do that" he said softly.

There were a few moments of silence as I didn't know how to respond.

"I really can't believe that I am talking to a ghost," he was wondering about our communication. He got up and collected the broken pieces of his talking gadget. Then sat back on the chair to face me – the radio.
I also didn't believe that I was talking to a human being.
"In your eyes, I am a ghost. But in my eyes, I am Chennamma who has special powers to control things around me without having a physical body," I said moving the sharp knife in the air in the kitchen which he wasn't aware of.
"That's the whole purpose of my visit. You have to understand that you cannot kill human beings. You have to leave this place.

This place is not for you," he said now holding the little bottle after fixing the talking gadget.
"And... I am back." Tom intervened. "Who are you talking to Aarav?"
"The horrifying night has finally transformed into a beautiful day. The sun is scattering its mild sunrays over the horizon to beautify our souls. I really think it's time to move out and dissolve in nature, Chennamma," he explained.
"What will you do if I don't go out?" I was almost bringing the knife to stab him from the back of his neck.

This time his look at the bottle was enough to make me weak. I think I was drifting into the bottle. The knife fell down making the noise, gaining his attention. He turned to look at the fallen knife and turned back to me.
"You can't be trusted anymore. I am sorry," he was completing the process.
I was shouting weekly "Wait. I didn't kill any human beings. They were all monsters. You should hear me out before you imprison me in that little bottle. I really don't want to lose the freedom which I earned after my death."
I was pleading with someone after a long time.
"What can justify killings?" he asked.
"What's wrong in killing the killers?" I retorted.
"But I am not a killer. Why did you try to kill me?" he asked.
I didn't have any clear spontaneous answer for that.
"You can do two things: Either imprison me in that little bottle forever by keeping my ghost mindset alive forever, or... free me into nature by having a discussion with me to understand what made me turn into this ghost you are talking to."

He was silent.

"So, what do you want to do? Imprison a ghost or free a spirit?" I asked once again.
"One's spirit is always free. Education is always better than a mere punishment for doing wrong. Tell me your story. I want to listen to you. What changed you into this?" Aarav said, stopping the process of imprisonment.

His voice was softening. Though he stopped the process of imprisonment, I didn't feel like trying to kill him again.

"Boss, I really don't understand how you are able to communicate with a ghost so freely as if it's your friend. And now you are asking it to tell its story. Are you trying to run a therapy over her?" Tom intervened.
"Don't pay attention to Tom's words. Just tell me your story, Chennamma," he asked in a soft voice.
Someone finally wanted to hear me out nearly after fifty years of my death. How weird!

"To know my story, we have to go back to the 1950s when I was rejoicing in my childhood," I said.

A curious man and his talking bot were ready to listen to a story told by a ghost in a haunted house on a hill. What a perfect setting for a storytelling session! An attentive listener always stimulates the speaker to speak with more energy.

"We are ready to devour every part of your story, Chennamma. Let's hear it out," said Tom.
I started to tell them my story.

PART TWO

Chapter 6: The Ghost's Therapy- My history- My early childhood

My life is like one day. As a child, I rose like the Sun in the early morning, serene and beautiful. As a teen, I was shining bright like the scorchy sun in the afternoon. As an adult, I was slowly exhausted like the sun of the evening, calming down again. As a middle-aged, I sank down only in the darkness. I was expecting that a new day would start soon but it never came. My story is like most of the stories of the girls of my time – like one day.

My story is set in 1950s. As far as the memories of my childhood go, one morning, I remember waking up fresh and strong. I thought the sun slowly stepped into the sky to scatter its gentle rays only to open my tiny eyes to reveal the face of the most beautiful person in this universe – my mother.

"Hey kiddo. You woke up? Why so early? Sleep. Sleep for some more time," she would tell me. But I was already stretching my body to relax the muscles, lying on the crutches on the floor.

Lying down like that, I just smiled at her, watching her go about her work. She looked fresh, which meant she had already taken a bath—implying she had also broomed the front yard, cleaned the house, and washed the dishes. Now she was busy picking out tiny stones from the rice to be cooked—so small they wouldn't be visible even under a microscope. Now and then, she walked into the kitchen and blew air through the windpipe to keep the stove burning. The daal was already cooking.

Though it was made of mud and had a tiled roof, my home was a decent one. I believed it was the most beautiful place on earth. It had a living room, a kitchen, some open space in the backyard with flowering trees and bathing arrangements, and a front yard with a small veranda where people could sit and talk. Beside our house, a few clusters of similar homes rested like lifelong friends. These clusters were surrounded by farmland, gentle hill terrains of barren land, and patches of dry forest. I felt it was the perfect setting to enjoy one's childhood.

Laying down, I asked my ma, "Maa, why didn't you wake me up early today?"
"Today is your fourth birthday, my little darling. So, I wanted to give you some rest. After growing up, you have to work all day like me. So, why don't you enjoy and chill on your special day?" she said smilingly.
"Maa, I will enjoy the day but I won't grow up. Who will do all these works everyday?" I said as a four year child.
"You know, four is the age when we almost start remembering our lives. So someday, you'll remember that your mom told you this. Every girl has to grow up, take care of her life, her home. And after some years, she has to marry, and look after her husband and children. That's how this world is designed. You should be ready for it, my sweetheart," she explained, with tiny fragments of tears in her eyes.
"But ma, why are tears rolling out of your eyes?"
"No, It's just because of the onions," she lied softly in the broad daylight. In reality, she was picking tiny stones from the rice, wasn't she?

In the fresh daylight pouring into our house through the windows on her face, I could see her dark and beautiful face. I think she was in the final year of her teenage days. Her face was as round as an orange, with small, almond shaped eyes which were shining due to faint tears. Her lips, nose, and eyes looked like delicate carvings, as if an expert had gently fitted them onto her orange shaped dusky face. God, she was beautiful – and there were quiet tears in her eyes.

"Maa, I know you're just picking the tiniest stones from the rice—there are no onions there. Don't lie. I won't marry and go anywhere. And if I do marry and take care of my man, when will I take care of you?" I said, "I don't want to marry and leave you or this place."
She smiled. "See? You're already talking like a grown-up. I think I should start looking for a match right away."
"Ammaa..." I shouted in sweet anger.
She explained patiently, "Don't worry, little darling. It'll take a few more years—maybe many—for your prince to find you. Until then, we have plenty of time to enjoy ourselves. Now quickly get up, let me give you a bath."

So, the day began with the splish-splash of water brought from the nearest lake and soapnuts. As I danced and made faces like a monkey, my mom would shout, "Chennamma, do you know your feet never stay in one place? They just move and move like a strong wind."

I would continue my free-spirited mischief, looked after by the most powerful person in the universe—someone who never scolded me, only gently corrected me, and never let even a single scratch befall me.

Once I was ready, she made me pray to God. She prayed along with me too. She always wished that all good things would happen to me—now and forever. I often wondered why she always prayed for me and never for herself. Then I realized: why would God pray for God? She was a God to me, because she never sacrificed anything in a way that made me feel like I was the reason for her pain. Instead, she always tried to be her best self, just to give me a beautiful life. She was the powerful source of life from whom I received my joy and nurture. Somehow, I felt she was eternal.

It was afternoon, the hour of the scorching sun. We were lying down after having our lunch and the sweet paayasam she had made for my birthday. Through the window beside us, we could see the blazing sun lashing its vanquishing heat onto the tranquil trees. While I was almost asleep—or so my mother thought—the only limitation to her strength, my father, returned home after nearly two days.

As he entered the front yard and washed his feet with water from the small container my mother always kept filled with lake water, she quietly got up, leaving me there to rest—thinking I was asleep. But I was watching everything. I think children always watch everything.

He sat silently in the living room.

"What happened?" she asked again.
"Rukmini, arrange some water for my bath," he ordered.
"I'll do that. But can't you hear my question? Where were you for the last two days?" she asked, a little louder.
"Is this how you speak to your husband who's just returned after two days?" he shouted.

"We were worried about you. Chennamma kept asking for you. There's hardly anything left at home to eat. Do you even know that?"
"Bear a girl child, tear a hole in the family's pocket, and then have the nerve to shout at me like this," he snapped, shooting a look at me as he began undressing for his bath.

Mother, who had already arranged hot water in a container in the backyard, asked, "Did you bring any money home? We need to buy groceries."
"Don't irritate me by asking about money every time you open your mouth. Things are terrible outside. There's a drought. The farmlands are as barren as you—unable to give me a male child," he said, cursing.
"First of all, you didn't bring any money. Then you shout at us, trying to blame us for the drought. If there were no women, who would give birth to men?" my mother shot back. She wasn't someone who got intimidated easily.
"Don't preach with your little dirty mouth. I won't hesitate to sell Chennamma if things get worse," he threatened.
"Remember this—I'll rip you apart if that day ever comes. Now tell me, where were you for the last two days?" she demanded.

I thought, maybe this is how women are supposed to look after their men.

He didn't respond for a while. Then, as my mother helped him bathe in the backyard, he slowly began to reveal the conversation he had with the people at the Gunj—the marketplace where he had gone to sell the harvest.

The conversation at Gunj as told by father:

I met many of my friends at the Gunj, including Nageshwar—after many years. The drought had affected our village, Kolluru, and hit many surrounding villages severely. The harvests were minimal. We sold what little we had for a meagre amount, and immediately Jogi Babu asked me to repay his debt. I couldn't repay the full amount but managed to settle fifty percent by giving him three rupees and fifty aanaas. I was left with one rupee and fifty aanaas. I kept the amount in my pocket, and just as I was about to leave, my old friends invited me to join them for a cup of tea at a nearby place.

The old lady placed some dry sticks into the fire and began making tea. Nageshwar started sharing details about his personal life.

Nageshwar looked gloomy. Even the hot tea couldn't reignite his lost enthusiasm. He was such a talkative friend who now looked lost.

Father: Hey Nageshwar, is everything alright? You seem a little lost.
Nageshwar: There's no such thing as 'alright' in a poor man's life. Some kind of mischief plays with our lives every single day.
Father: What is it now? What mischief has taken hold of you this time that made you so gloomy?
Nageshwar: Roshayya, what can I say—this mischief has wreaked havoc in our lives. It's not mischief, it's a curse. My little Lakshmi, whom I once thought to be a blessing, has turned into a curse in disguise. Ever since she became a woman, I've been facing extreme hardships. I tried to find a suitable groom, but couldn't find any. Where do young men these days become eligible for marriage? They can barely earn enough for themselves.

So, I received offers from older men in their forties and fifties. At least they had their own shelters, and I felt that was better. Though Lakshmi wasn't interested, we thought it wouldn't be a bad idea to marry her off to an old landlord—he even promised to give us some money in return. We accepted the money and fixed the wedding forty-five days later. I used the amount to pay off old debts and tend to the fields. But as you can see, the drought swallowed everything. I spent it all for nothing.

Lakshmi, who was used to praying to Durga at the small temple on the hill beside the lake, went there a day before her wedding. As the day wore into night, she didn't return. My son and I waited anxiously, then went to find her. We saw the beautifully adorned goddess Durga in the temple, and beside it, Lakshmi's footwear—right at the edge of the steep hill leading to the lake. But Lakshmi wasn't there. Our hearts pounded. We searched everywhere through the night, but couldn't find her.

When morning light struck the lake, we found her body. My twelve-year-old little girl, beautifully dressed, without a single bruise—lay there, lifeless. I had no words. We took her out and performed the final rites.

She left the world, but her curse remained. The landlord, upon hearing what happened, demanded his money back. But we don't have it. He's taken my son as a slave until I repay the debt. With this drought and misfortune, I don't think I'll ever be able to bring him back. God shouldn't give a girl child even to one's enemies."

Nageshwar ended his sad story while sipping his last of the tea. I was listening intently to his story.

Nageshwar asked me "What about your personal life? How's life treating you?"

I told him, "I have one daughter who is around 4 years."

"Argh, that's a beautiful phase of having a girl child," Nageshwar said, "but slowly, as she grows up, the blessing turns into a terrible curse. Believe me, I have gone through it."

"I wanted to get rid of her on her first day. But I couldn't," my father said.

"Even I wanted to get rid of my little Lakshmi on her very first day, as per my mother's instruction," Nageshwar added. "But I didn't have the heart to harm her. She was so beautiful. If we don't kill the love on the first day, it blossoms into a full forest—and someday, it destroys us."

"But I had the hands to kill mine on her first day. Rukmini was lying in labor pains, having labored alone through the night in our home, she finally delivered. I rushed in to see the exhausted mother and the crying baby beside her. I soon realized she was a girl. Fear flooded my body and mind. Careful not to raise suspicion in my wife's mind, I slowly picked up the crying baby, studying her tiny features as if trying to soothe her. I walked with her here and there, and finally into the kitchen, where I found some water in a vessel. I slowly bent down and immersed her in the vessel to suffocate her—and the crying stopped.

My wife shouted weakly from inside, "Why has the baby suddenly stopped crying? What's happening?"

I said, "The baby is falling asleep."

She didn't believe me. Somehow, even in those painful moments, she got to her feet and rushed to the kitchen. The little girl was bubbling in the water. "What the hell are you doing? Have you gone mad?" she screamed, hitting me hard with a dining plate. She quickly pulled the baby out and began drying her, checking if she was still alive. Unfortunately, the baby was still breathing. She set the baby aside and returned to me—only to kick me a hundred times, even during her pain. I was helpless in that moment of weakness and couldn't retaliate. She threw me out of the house and locked the doors."

Sipping the last of the tea from my cup, I said, "I had the hands to kill mine on her first day, but I couldn't complete the task. I'm afraid something similar will happen to me, just like it happened to you."

Before leaving, Nageshwar said, "Be careful."

Conversation at Gunj ends.

"I parted from him in one of my lowest moods. Even tea couldn't lift my spirits. On the way, I came across a liquor shop, spent a few aanas, and drank so much that I forgot everything. I woke up after one and a half days. Now, I'm left with just half an aana," my father told my mother.

My mother watched him as he finished his bath, listening quietly to his story. Once he was inside the house and dressed, she asked, "Give me those remaining aanas—I need to buy groceries." He hesitated. She snatched the aanas from him.

While pretending to sleep and overhear their conversation as a four-year-old, I realized that my mother never left me alone with my father. Somehow, though I didn't understand the meaning of "getting rid of someone" at that age, I remember bubbling under the water on my first day—or maybe I was dreaming.

If I were to title my childhood story, it would be: A Saviour, a Child, and a Killer. The saviour is my mother. I am the child. And my father—the killer—was the one who always wanted to end my life.

Chapter 7: My Childhood

I was five. Green fields stretched across the entire world—or at least as far as my eyes could see. As the hot summer winds blew, I played under the trees near a farm with other children. Most of us wore lahengas and jackets, as worn out as our sun-faded faces. Sometimes, we played on swings we made ourselves using ropes or our mothers' sarees. Our shrill, excited voices reassured our parents working in the fields that we were nearby and safe. After many arguments with my father—who was absolutely certain our suffering was because of a girl child—my mother finally began working on her own, though the earnings were meagre.

As I was lost in play with the other children, I suddenly saw my father's face—it was like that of a lone snake in a garden of flowers. For the first time, he was smiling at me. He raised his hand and signalled for me to come closer. I froze, unsure of what to do.

My little friends, noticing him, nudged me with mischievous grins.

"Your father's here," one whispered, giggling.

"Go, he's calling you," another teased, their voices light and unaware of the weight I felt.

Though hesitant at first, I didn't think too much about it. I knew my mother wouldn't have liked me going near him, but something in his smile—so unfamiliar, so strange—pulled me in. I took a few cautious steps toward him, my heart thudding like a drum made of fear and curiosity.

As I went near him, he smiled and said, “It’s so good to see you playing with your friends.” I smiled back, unsure of what to say. My face must have looked like the marigold flowers blooming in the farm.

“Have you heard there’s a big fair happening in our neighbouring village, Ponnur?” he continued.

Now I felt compelled to respond. “What’s a fair, Father?” I asked, my voice filled with innocent curiosity.

“Oh, little one, don’t you know what a fair is? It’s a place where children see big marketplaces, huge swings to play on, giant wheels to ride, crowds of people everywhere, delicious pakoras and sugar candies to eat, and colourful balloons to play with. Oh! The fair is such a beautiful place.”

I was enchanted by his vivid description. He had never spoken to me like that before. I hesitated for a few moments, then asked, “Can I go there with my mother?”

“Yes, you can—but it’s closing today. And by the time you go with her, since she’s working in the faraway fields, I think you’ll be very delayed. The day will end soon.”

Hit by the feeling of missing the fair, I didn’t know what to say.

He broke my awkward silence. “If you’re really interested, I can take you there and bring you back home safely.”

I wasn't worried about getting back safely. I was more concerned about the pakoras—they sounded delicious the way he described them. "Will you buy me pakoras there?"

He smiled. "Sure, Chennamma."

We started our walk across the never-ending fields that seem to sprawl throughout the earth. Sometimes we walked beneath the tall trees; sometimes we paused to watch the colourful, chirping birds. Those sights touched my heart, but bore a stark contrast with the silent relationship between me and my father. But, I somehow believed him this time. Maybe, the goat only trusts the butcher.

With a few more twists and turns, I was finally there—the fair. I had thought that only fields and trees covered the entire planet, but here was a vast exhibition of human beings sprawled across the plain lands. I had never seen such a huge crowd gathered in one place.

My eyes first landed on the giant wheel and the awestruck expressions of the people riding it. Their shrill voices still echo in my mind. Then there were merry-go-rounds with children my age riding them, their faces beaming with joy.

Just as my father had described, there were pakoras, sugar candies, and colourful balloons. I looked at the pakoras, then at my father—and he understood. He brought me a packet full of them. I munched on them, wide-eyed, taking in the grand spectacle.

There were some tents with other events going on. I wondered what was going on inside them. But, one had to pay to enter them, and I didn't have any money. Then, there was a big bazaar where sellers displayed all kinds of things: household utensils, toys I longed for, delicious sweets, and a variety of clothes. I wanted to have all of them.

As I was walking, lost in the sea of this fair, I turned around – only to realize that my father was no longer with me. I turned my head around in full circle and scanned almost all the shops around me; I couldn't find him anywhere. I searched for some more time and then the hope died. Finally, I felt like I was deserted in this sea of unknown people. The only person who I hardly knew had vanished. Now, it was only me, my naked feet, and a packet of pakoras.

I didn't know what to do—I didn't even know the way back home. And out of nowhere, I saw two strange-looking men approaching me. One of them pointed at me and said to the other, "That's the girl."

Somehow, my instinct screamed that they were harmful, and I started to run. I ran faster than the spinning merry-go-rounds and the giant wheel, still clutching the pakoras in my hand. But they kept up with my pace.

Just as they were about to catch me, I crawled inside one of the tents; they couldn't crawl in like I did because of their sizes. As I crept all the way in, I realized that I had landed into a circus filled with animals and human performers doing incredible stunts. Humans were swinging from high ropes, dogs were walking on rolling balls, elephants wore hats and goggles, shaking heads like human beings.

For a moment, I forgot about the two people chasing me. The fair felt like a circus, everyone tried to perform their best. And my father was the best performer out of everyone.

From the corner of my eye, I saw the two men entering the tent through the main entry, they must have paid the entry fee. Sensing that they were coming near me, I again slipped out of the tent by crawling out. This time, they were left inside the tent.

As the day's light was slowly fading, I then crawled into another tent out of sheer curiosity to explore what was going on there.

Unlike the circus, this tent was silent. People just sat on the chairs which were neatly organized and looked at the stage on which a person was giving some speech.

He was saying something like, "Education illuminates the darkness in our lives and brings us into the light of knowledge and peace. With education, we learn that we don't need to hurt one another to be happy. Any education that teaches us to shun others for their beliefs or practices is nothing but brainwashing. And the kind of education that tells us to forbid a woman from doing a man's job, from getting educated, from standing on her own and growing like a beautiful tree—that kind of education is utter trash."

The once-silent room suddenly erupted into thunderous applause.

As I sat in the last rows, trying not to get caught for sneaking in without a ticket, I tried to catch a glimpse of the gentleman who had given that powerful speech—he sounded truly fascinating. Just as I was about to see him clearly, a hand clamped over my mouth and another slid around my waist. I was lifted and slowly taken outside.

“Give a woman the freedom she deserves”—that was the last line I heard from the speaker, as my heart pounded in fear while I was being taken away.

As soon as we stepped out of the tent, I bit the hand covering my mouth with all the strength I could muster. He screamed in pain, and I took off running again. But as the day darkened, I lost the advantage of the crowd’s presence. One of the men was able to reach me, gave me a sudden shove while I was running, and I fell hard onto the ground.

I turned from where I lay and saw the two lurking shadows closing in. I shut my eyes tightly in fear. Just as they were about to grab my arm, a digging bar came crashing down on them from a figure whose shadow stirred something deep in me.

They were struck so fiercely, they didn’t dare return. As the figure stepped into the fading light, recognition bloomed. It was my mother.

Gasping and sweating heavily, and holding me close to her heart, she began the walk back to our house. With the occasional scolding for not telling her about coming to the fair, she kept reassuring me that everything was alright, and that I didn’t need to be afraid anymore.

My heart, which had been pounding in fear, finally began to calm beside this towering, god-like figure. From the safety of her arms, I looked up at her face after glancing at the starlit sky—and in that moment, I felt she must truly be a god. The invincible.

That night, we went home and had our dinner. She put me to bed and waited for a while. I slept—or rather, I pretended to, as I had many times before.

My father finally returned home in a drunken state; he must have been feeling triumphant, thinking he had finally gotten rid of me.

But the moment his eyes fell on me, his intoxicated joy dimmed—though he didn't show it, careful not to arouse my mother's suspicion. A deafening silence lingered between them for the rest of the evening.

My father had his dinner, and I somehow felt he was even more inebriated afterward. Within minutes, he was asleep—almost like an unconscious man. My mother cast a few cautious glances around the room, hurried outside to check for any signs of people nearby, and, finding no one, closed the door.

She walked over to my father, gave him one final look, then took a pillow and pressed it firmly against his face to suffocate him. His hands tried to rise in resistance, but they were tied with ropes—so were his legs. All he could do was attempt to lift his face, but he couldn't, not against the violent pressure of my mother's determined hands.

Within moments, he was gone.

The saviour became the killer—by killing the killer who wanted to kill the child. It was a strange twist in our story to end the day. And, as the day finally came to a close, I slept peacefully without any fear.

Chapter 8: The Phase of just me and my mother

After my father's untimely passing in his sleep, many relatives, neighbours, and friends came to console us. They were worried about how we—two females—could live without a man's support. As a child, I didn't understand those words of consolation, but they began to make sense as I grew up and saw the world in a different light.

Now, our living room, kitchen, backyard, and front yard—which together made up our entire house—had only us. My mother never showed it on her face, but at times I could sense her worry about managing everything alone. A widow with a daughter is seen as a burden, a disgrace to society. She was in her twenties now, which made her more vulnerable in certain ways: men would see her as prey, and women would see her as a bad omen.

She couldn't go anywhere without me because I was just seven. And I followed her everywhere—like her shadow.

Soon, I noticed that my mother's face, neck, and hands were bare, stripped of all her ornaments. I asked her, "Amma, where is all your jewellery?"

"I've turned them into food supplies, dear... and maybe a bit of education for you," she replied gently.

I understood food—but not education.

For a few days, we had enough food to get by. Soon, my mother resumed work in the surrounding fields and houses. I followed her wherever she went. She often scolded me, urging me to make some friends and play with them instead of clinging to her saree's palloo like a faithful dog.

So I tried to find friends whenever I could—and became a faithful dog whenever I couldn't.

As I played with girls my age, I watched my mother toiling under the hot sun. Her hair—now about nine inches long after being clean-shaven during my father's funeral—was tied behind her back and shone like a black diamond. I saw her carrying pots of water from the nearby lake to our home, which wasn't actually all that near.

I also saw her face remain expressionless in response to the taunts from the village folk—remarks like, "Look at the woman who swallowed her man at such a young age," or "She's still in her prime... maybe I could offer her some help."

I knew she heard every word. But she never let it show on her face. She never let it matter.

I watched her checking the boxes in the kitchen to see how much money was left—because that's where it was usually kept. Sometimes, I caught a glimpse of fear on her face, though she never revealed it to me. Years later, I came to understand that empty kitchen boxes can stir a terrifying feeling in a mother's heart.

I saw her break into tears at times—never in front of me—and then gather herself again, resolute in making things work. I watched her in fascination, just as I watched the stars in the night sky.

One day, as we sat in the moonlight, relishing each other's company, she told us that we would be doing things differently from tomorrow. She said she was running out of work, as a drought had taken over the village, and that we would soon be running out of money too.

I, being a child of seven, didn't understand what a drought was—but 'doing things differently' sounded like an adventure.

The next day, I woke up to see an old lady in my room. I wasn't afraid of her sudden appearance—her presence was oddly comforting—but I was frightened because I couldn't find my mother anywhere. I asked the old lady to help me, and she agreed in a soft, gentle voice—on one condition: I had to close my eyes for a couple of seconds.

I closed my eyes for what felt like an eternity. When I was told to open them, I saw something entirely different. The frail, drooping figure was gone. In her place stood a woman—erect, graceful, and radiant. Her dark skin had softened into a warm glow, and the scornful lines on her face had melted into a smile so familiar I could recognize it from miles away.

Her saree now clung to her with quiet elegance, her eyes sparkled with fierce determination, and her posture spoke of someone who had shed sorrow and stepped into strength.

Recognition dawned. The old lady was my mother—in disguise, reborn in a new avatar.

"What is this new avatar, Amma?"

"I don't have a job now because of the drought. I'm figuring out new ways to earn money."

"But how will you earn money with this new avatar? Who would give a job to an old lady?"

"I'll show you how to earn money, not tell you—so shh, your mouth," she said, placing the finger of her right hand gently on my lips.

"But Amma, there's no drought outside. The fields are green, and the lake has water," I said. I was seven, almost turning eight now, proudly displaying my growing intelligence through my questions.

My mother, almost reading my mind, answered after a pause.

"This draught is different. It is a draught of goodness. Child, as you grow into a woman, you should know—A young, beautiful widow is dangerous in the eyes of society. An aging, broken woman is invisible."

"So... you want to be invisible? Why so suddenly, Amma?"

"Because the landlord of the fields where I worked made a sudden entry yesterday while we were working. He asked me to come to his wooden cabin at the far end of the field to 'talk.' Though I sensed danger, I went. He attempted rape. But I flung him to one side of the room and walked out."

I didn't understand much, but I knew that rape meant something really bad. Suddenly, the drought, the makeover, the idea of 'doing things differently'—everything made sense to me. I didn't dare ask about rape any further.

"What now, Amma?"

She showed me her makeover kit—soot, oil, ragged clothes, and hair whitener, which she must have invented overnight. Even my already worn-out dress was replaced with one even more tattered one.

And then, in the early morning light, we headed to Durga's temple, almost near the next village.

On the way, she poured quiet wisdom into my ears:

"Till the world learns how to respect a woman, let's look ugly. Let's walk like we have nothing and no one will want to take anything from us."

As the sun was about to rise completely, we traversed the fields and the kacha road of our village in a rickshaw and finally reached the temple. The rickshaw puller, Anjaneyulu, was more than happy to drop us there for a few aanas. Since a few aanas were enough for him to stay intoxicated and indulge his senses, he became our regular driver to various places in the future.

Soon, we sat at the footsteps of the temple after our makeovers. My mother now looked like my old grandmother—her hair turned white, her back bent, and her clothes ragged.

I was no longer beautiful either, with my big front teeth, one eye larger and oddly shaped than the other, and even a slight hunchback. We were certain no one would dare consider adopting me.

But soon, we faced an unexpected problem—competition from other beggars. Still, my mother begged, borrowed, and even stole a spot on the steps near the temple entrance to begin our begging affair.

The first day wasn't bad—we earned almost as much as my mother would have made working in the fields. Gradually, we began to appreciate our acting skills. In our free time, we observed other beggars. Their ways of appealing to the nobler motives of temple visitors were fascinating.

They would say:

"Please offer something, your children at home will rest peacefully," to parents.

"Please offer something, we haven't eaten in ages. You'll go to heaven for feeding these hungry stomachs," to the elderly.

"Please offer something, you'll soon get a nice husband or wife," to the unmarried.

And so on and so forth.

But my mother had better ideas.

We began to take note of the wealthy, kind men and women—recognizing them by their ornaments, clothing, and landlord-like mannerisms.

As we were heading back home in the evening, just before the sun was about to set, Anjaneyulu—though a bit drunk—started speaking to us, something we never expected.

"How was your day?" he asked, pulling the rickshaw with his old, frail body.

"It was good," my mother replied, a bit hesitant.

"You should see that temple on Fridays—the crowd gets even bigger."

"Okay," my mother said.

"In fact, you should go to different places on different days, wherever people gather."

"Hmm," my mother murmured, making a mental note.

Soon, he dropped us at our house. My mother gave him two aanas and asked, "What would you say if someone asked where we went?"

With a smile on his wrinkled face, he replied, "To a field in the adjacent village where her aunt works."

"Good. Take this," she said, handing him one more aana. His old face lit up with a beaming smile.

We somehow trusted him—he was too old, too quiet, and didn't talk much to anyone in the village.

Later, we began using old Anjaneyulu to buy us some groceries—meagre ones, just enough so people wouldn't suspect our suddenly increasing earnings.

Finally, it was rest time for the tired labour duo. We chatted about our day, laughed at how people melted with a few praises and good wishes and ended up offering money, and at how other beggars came up with new schemes. No matter how grand their tricks were, the grandma-granddaughter duo remained an outstanding pair. We made ambitious plans to be present at important places during festivals and special occasions.

It was Friday evening, and the sun was just about to set in the west. The crowd at the temple was slowly thinning. A wealthy lady and a child, maybe her granddaughter—who resembled my mother and me—were walking past us. My mother called out, "Amma."

She didn't stop, but her daughter tugged her hand and pointed toward me, lying on the floor, almost unconscious, with flies buzzing across my face. My mother, while shooing the flies away with a cloth, began to shed tears.

The wealthy mother asked, "What happened?"

My grandmother began, "Where should I start? My daughter, whose husband passed away a few years ago, died recently—leaving me with this hunchback child. I'm an old woman. Where can I earn enough to feed and care for her? She hasn't eaten anything since morning and suddenly collapsed. I don't know what to do. God is testing me harshly in this old age."

Though I was pretending to be unconscious, I was mind-blown by my mother's spontaneous acting.

"Take this and get her checked at a hospital," the woman said, handing over a five-rupee note. It was the first time I saw a five-rupee note, even if only from the corner of my eye.

But my mother didn't take it. She kept weeping. "What should I do? I feel completely helpless without my daughter. What will happen to this little girl in the future?"

"Don't worry. Durga is there to take care of everyone. I understand how you feel—I'm here with my granddaughter too, after my daughter passed away. Keep faith, and you'll be alright. Take this." She removed a hefty golden bangle from her wrist and gave it to my mother, along with the five-rupee note.

My mother didn't take it immediately. But as the other grandmother insisted, she finally accepted it, saying, "You have a heart like the rivers Ganga and Yamuna combined. May you always live happily, and may your granddaughter grow into a beautiful young lady and find a good husband." She spoke those words straight from her heart.

Without wasting time, we left the place. Behind us, we could hear an old man shouting at the kind woman for giving away her golden bangle. "They may be fraudsters!" he yelled.

She turned to look at us—but we were already gone. She might have felt deceived, just as her husband feared. We never saw her kind face again, and we never knew what happened afterward.

Back in our original worn-out clothes, changed from the ragged ones, old Anjaneyulu cruised us back home swiftly through the thick evening air. He dropped us off happily, having received his share of five aanas—enough for him to drink till his neck and fall flat on his face on the road.

We eagerly opened the sack to check the day's earnings: many aanas, a glorious five-rupee note, and a glittering, heavy golden bangle. Amma tried to guess its weight just by lifting it—perhaps 60 grams, almost the same as the one Durga is adorned with.

"Sixty grams! Are we going to be rich?" I shouted in joy, my happiness overflowing at the sight of our newly earned treasure.

But my mother didn't share the same excitement. Her eyes didn't shine like they usually did after one of our conspiracies.

"What's the matter, Amma?"

"She was a good lady. I never wanted to deceive good people," she said, tears flowing down her cheeks.

"Amma, you said that lady had a heart like Ganga and Yamuna combined—and now your eyes are like Ganga and Yamuna combined. Please don't cry," I said, trying to comfort her.

"Her husband must be scolding her right now."

"She was as great as you. She'll manage her husband," I said with a sly smile, thinking of the playful quarrels between my mother and my late father.

She didn't stop crying for a while—until I said:

"Amma, think of her like Durga. Durga came to save us from poverty. Durga will save her too."

Amma finally smiled through her tears. "You're learning so many words," she said.

"Tell me about it! I'm working with the best crime partner in the world—my mother. How could I not learn at least these many words to survive... or to make my lovely Amma laugh?"

At last, Amma laughed fully, pulling me into her arms and swaying with me like sunflowers dancing in the wind on a sunny day.

We had our dinner.

"Rukmini, so what's next?" I asked.

"Chennamma, I know what to do from here. You sleep for now," my mother said.

I believed her completely. And for the first time in a long while, I slept peacefully—because I could feel the peace and relief in my mother too.

The next day, we set out for a completely new village, carrying some dazzling new clothes in our sack. This time, my mother's plan was to pose as if we belonged to a royal family. Anjaneyulu, already briefed on the plan, took us straight to the village blacksmith, who was quite well-known.

We quickly changed our get-ups. My mother transformed into a wealthy old woman, and I became her rich, spoiled granddaughter.

We entered the blacksmith's shop where the blacksmith was busy with some calculations.

"I need your help, as the blacksmith in our village is out of town," my mother told him in her authoritative tone.

"Tell me, ma'am, how can I help you?" the blacksmith asked, trying to gauge her background by observing her attire and imitation ornaments.

"I have five daughters, all married. Now that my husband is no more, they're fighting over my property—while I'm still alive."

"How sad," he said.

"Grandmother, I want to leave this dirty place immediately—it smells like iron!" I shouted, scrunching my nose at the blacksmith's workshop.

"You little miss problem-finder, be quiet for a while," she scolded, then turned to the blacksmith. "Please don't mind her. She's spoiled by her mother. Thinks she's the queen of the world."

"But madam, how can I help you?"

"Since I don't want to write my property in their names while I'm alive, I want to divide one of my gold jewels equally among them—to keep them quiet for now."

"Oh, that's quite thoughtful," he said.

"Grandmother, how long will you take? I'll throw these things off the table!" I said, pointing to his tools like a disgruntled child.

"Eh! Will you stay silent for a few minutes?" my grandmother snapped.

"She's like a little tornado," the blacksmith chuckled, glancing at me. "Tell me quickly—what's the work?"

My mother took out the golden bangle. "This was given to me by my mother. I want to divide it into five parts and give one to each of my daughters."

The blacksmith took the bangle and began examining it. But before he could study it too closely, I created more nuisance to distract him and speed things up. Though he seemed a bit skeptical about how we came to possess such a large gold bangle, our devious plan left him no time to dwell on it. My antics made him work faster.

My grandmother sighed, "I don't understand how daughters these days can be so cruel. Fighting over property while I'm still breathing!"

"No, madam, maybe it's not your daughters—it could be their husbands, your sons-in-law. They're often the ones hungry to devour property," the blacksmith said while melting the bangle.

"I don't know. And they leave their spoiled kids with me as if I have some magic formula to manage them," she added, pointing at me as I continued grumbling.

"Old lady, finish it fast! I want to go on a horse ride after this!" I shouted.

"You keep your mouth shut! I don't know what I'll do if you open it again!" she shouted back.

Naturally, I had to be furious. I began pulling down the hanging garlands at the entrance of the blacksmith's shop.

"No, no!" he cried, rushing to stop me and speeding up his work.

He quickly handed over six gold biscuits of 10 grams each to my mother. She paid him a decent amount, and we walked out.

The blacksmith must have finally breathed a sigh of relief. Thanks to my mother's brilliant plan—and my timely nuisance—he never once doubted how we came to possess that golden bangle.

The next step involved a few more dubious acts. Anjaneyulu took us to several other villages, where we sold the golden biscuits—citing various reasons: a dead husband, an ailing father, a relative's operation, and so on. With each act, I felt we were performing better. Eventually, we were relieved to have sold all the biscuits.

By the end of it all, my mother was left with four hundred rupees—a significant amount.

Soon, our house began to smell of raw mangoes and chilli powder. I wondered what Amma was up to this time. I wanted to ask, but the sight said it all—she was about to launch a new business venture: pickles.

Raw mangoes were chopped into small pieces, mixed with chilli powder, salt, mustard seeds, and just the right amount of edible oil, releasing a tangy, citrusy aroma—her new product: Raw Mango Pickles. Packed into two or three ceramic jars, the pickles became our companions on journeys to various bazaars where we sold them.

Note: even though we were on the verge of starting a great enterprise, we still made sure to look as shabby as possible. Riding in Anjaneyulu's rickshaw from one market to another, passing through fields, calculating income, expenditure, and profits—we were having the time of our lives.

Then, when I turned nine, an idea struck my mother's mind: my schooling. But there was a problem—the nearest school was in the adjacent village. We sat thoughtfully, wondering what to do. A smile lit up her face, and she said, "Hey little one, don't you worry. I'll drop you at school every day and go sell pickles. I'll return by the time school ends to take you back."

And so, a new companion entered my life—a small school bag with a slate and pencil, slung across my shoulder.

Every morning, we battled with time—cleaning the house, getting ready, and cooking—before school began. Somehow, fetching water from the nearby lake and buying groceries became easier, thanks to Anjaneyulu, whom we used whenever needed.

Even now, I distinctly remember those school days.

Chapter 9: My School Days

My school was an old building in a dilapidated condition, with ample space around it. On the first day we visited, we arrived a bit early and saw children playing and laughing out loud. The tan-tan-tan of the school bell made everyone stand in straight lines for the morning prayers. My mother and I stood watching quietly.

Soon after the prayers, the students scrambled like ants into their respective classrooms. We sat on benches outside the headmaster's cabin, waiting. Before long, we were called in and stepped through the small wooden doors.

The headmaster was a kind old man, seated on his chair as we stood before him. I remember their conversation to some extent—it went like this:

Mother: Namaste, Sir, she said, joining her palms.

HM: Namaste. Tell me, how can I help you?

Mother: Sir, my name is Rukmini. I want to get my daughter admitted to your school.

The headmaster looked at me through his spectacles, studying me carefully.

HM: What is her age? Has she had any basic education so far?

Mother: She's nine, about to turn ten. I haven't been able to get her any education till now, Sir.

The headmaster nodded thoughtfully and turned to me.

HM: What is your name?
Me: Chennamma.
HM: Where are you coming from?
Me: Nearby village, Sir—Kolluru.
HM: Can you name five villages near yours?
I rattled off the names effortlessly, having travelled to many places with my mother.
Me: Povvur, where melas happen every year; Ranganayakagudem, famous for the Durga temple; Raikoor, where there's a big goldsmith's shop...

I was getting excited, listing more, when I caught a look from my mother that told me to shut up.

HM: *Wow, you know so many villages—you know more than I do! Rukmini, why do you want to send your daughter to school?*
Mother: *Sir, I want her to learn to read and write. That way, she'll understand the world better. I want her to become intelligent.*

The headmaster was silent for a few moments.

HM: *Chennamma, at school, we'll tell you many stories—and you'll learn to speak, read, and write about them. Is that alright?*

I was quiet for a moment. My mother nudged me gently, and I said, *"Okay, Sir."*

He noted down our details and asked my mother to send me to school the next day.

On the way back, Amma expressed her happiness by buying me some jalebis, wooden toys, and a new slate.

I was happy for a while—but I was also scared. School felt like an unknown world I was about to step into.

****

The next day, my mother left me at school. I entered the classroom and saw my classmates—some younger than me, some older. We were all seated on the floor. Then began the rigorous training: stories, riddles, speaking, reading, and writing. The way our teacher narrated the stories—and the stories themselves—fascinated me.

"I have four legs. I cannot walk. But you can sit on me. Who am I?" he would ask.

We'd think for a few moments and then shout the answer together: "Chair!"

"I am an animal with four legs. I give sweet milk for everyone to drink. I say 'mow'. Who am I?"

"A goat?"

"No."

"A cow?"

"Yes, very good!"

And then came the poems of Vemana. One that we effortlessly remembered went like this:

Salt and camphor appear the same to the eye, but taste vary differently. Likewise, all people may look the same, but some are nobler than others. Listen to me, O Vemana.

Then came the turn of the stories—the tale of two brothers.

Elder Brother: *Father gave us only one cow before passing away. It's now our responsibility to take care of it.*
Younger Brother (who was a bit slow in worldly affairs): *Okay, brother.*
Elder Brother: *I'll take care of its body, and everything related to the body is mine. You take care of its head, and everything related to it is yours.*
So the younger brother was deceived. He was only there to feed the cow, while the elder one milked it and took all the milk. The younger brother couldn't say anything. Soon, he too got married, just like the elder one.
His new wife, noticing the unfairness, devised a plan. The next day, the younger brother began beating the cow's face instead of feeding it. When the elder brother asked why, the younger one replied:
Younger Brother: *The cow's head is mine. I can do whatever I wish with it.*
Elder Brother: *Don't do that—it'll die!*
Younger Brother: *Then what's the use of a cow's head that only takes and gives nothing in return?*
Elder Brother: I get what you're saying, brother. From now on, let's both look after the cow and share the milk equally.
At last, the elder brother said what he should have said long ago.

Then came the letters—to read from books and to write on the slate. My teacher used to say,

"The moment you can read a letter, you begin to read the world. The moment you can write a letter, you begin to express yourself to anyone, anywhere—and your words will live on for generations. So, children, wear torn clothes if you must, but buy a good book. It will guide you to earn all the beautiful things in the world someday."

One of the students stood up and asked, "What are the beautiful things, if not clothes?"

The teacher smiled and replied,

"Beautiful things come without a price—but with a lot of effort. Some of the most beautiful things are strong family bonds and friendships where people care for and love each other, the intellect to earn money with ease, and the mindset to stay happy no matter what."

We were all soaking in the knowledge and relishing it. I could feel my intellect expanding through this kind of education.

Always lost in awe of the raw mangoes hanging from the trees, I noticed that my mother always bought them from the Gunj—the marketplace. After almost three years of schooling and two years of observing those mangoes closely, I finally realized something: my mother was spending more money buying raw mangoes from the Gunj.

When I questioned her about it, she simply said, "That's the only way to buy. You can't purchase directly from farmers—landlords will get angry."

I was dissatisfied with that answer, especially coming from my very brave mother—a bold entrepreneur of her time.

Then something happened—something we knew about but had never cared to think about for a long time. A light bleeding, severe stomach pain, occasional cramps, and mood swings made me reclusive for a while. My mood swings especially bothered my mother.

It was morning, and the sun had just begun to shine like a golden plate in the sky. I was walking around haphazardly, unable to focus on any of my tasks.

Narrowing her eyes with suspicion, Amma asked, "What's wrong with you today?"

I grumbled, "Nothing. Maybe I don't like the way the sun is shining today."

"Oh? So you don't like the way the sun is shining today? Hey Sun, can you shine differently on my little one, please?" Amma said, speaking to the sun in a playful, pleading tone.

"Amma, please let me be. Everything is annoying today. Even the breeze is blowing in a stupid way!"

With a raised eyebrow, Amma replied, "Now you have problems with the breeze too? Poor thing—it's just doing its job. Did someone tease you at school? Steal your mango? Call you a baby?"

I crossed my arms and shouted, "No! I'm not a baby!"

"Hmm... that confirms it."

"Confirms what?" I demanded.

"You've started your periods, haven't you?"

I froze for a moment—like a thief caught in broad daylight. Then I tried to defend myself.

“What?! No! Never! I don’t even know what that is!”

Amma laughed. “Oh really? So you’re angry at the sun and the wind for no reason? And you’ve been sighing like a sad cat all morning. Come here.”

She reached out to me, but I stepped back.

“No. I don’t want to talk about it—it’s embarrassing.”

Amma let a soft smile spread across her lips. “Oh, my little sweet dove, why are you embarrassed? It just means you’re growing up. It happens to every woman. Even me!”

I wrinkled my nose. “You too?”

“Of course! What do you think? That I came into this world as a full-grown woman?”

I couldn’t say anything. I looked down at the ground, still unsure.

“Amma... I thought maybe I did something wrong.”

Amma pulled me close and hugged me tightly, stroking my hair.

“Chennamma, no, my love. You haven’t done anything wrong. This isn’t a curse or a punishment. It’s just nature. Proof that you’re strong. Proof that you’re becoming a woman. Proof that someday, you’ll be even stronger than me.”

With my head muffled against Amma's shoulder, I whispered, "Amma, I think I'm already stronger. I may not be stronger than you, but I can feel the strength."

Amma laughed. "Come now. Let me make something delicious for you—before you start yelling at the trees next."

I groaned a little but followed her inside. I smiled, knowing that my mother would always be by my side.

And the pain—which turned into sweet pain because of Amma's company—finally vanished in a few days. Life returned to normal.

My school and my mother's pickle business resumed. But my mind kept circling back to one thing—the purchase of raw mangoes only from the Gunj. My growing intellect made me question: how could a farmer who grows mangoes on his own trees not be allowed to sell them directly to anyone he wishes?

Each time my mother bought raw mangoes from the Gunj, I silently observed.

Then an opportunity struck when my mother said, "Hey Chennamma, today you go with Anjaneylu and get the raw mangoes from the Gunj. I have some work to finish at home."

I set off with Anjaneylu in his rickshaw. On the way to the Gunj, I noticed some mango fields. I asked Anjaneylu to stop and take me to the farmer of that field.

He was skeptical. As he guided me to the farmer's dilapidated house, he asked, "Chennamma, are you sure about what you're doing?"

"Yes!" I said.

Soon, our rickshaw stopped outside the farmer's house. I got down, walked to the main door, and called out.

A wrinkled-faced farmer and his wife, both in their mid-forties, came out.

The farmer smiled and asked, "Hey girl, what do you want? Why have you come here?"

"Hello sir, I need some raw mangoes to make pickles."

"Oh! Our fields produce very tangy mangoes—perfect for pickles. Wait, I'll give you some," the farmer's wife said joyfully.

"But I need more. Maybe five bags full," I said.

"But we can't give five bags just like that. You're a young girl who reminds us of our daughter, so we thought we could give you a few," the farmer replied.

"But sir, I'll pay you for the mangoes."

"Oh child, no, no. You can't buy mangoes from here. You can only buy them from the Gunj," the farmer's wife said with a weak smile.

"My mother and I usually buy from the Gunj, but the price is much higher there. I want to buy directly from you at a cheaper rate—and still pay you more than what you get from the Gunj sellers. Tell me, what price do they pay you per bag?"

"We get 10 aanas per bag," the farmer said hesitantly.

"I'll pay you 15 aanas per bag," I said, knowing that we paid 25 aanas per bag at the Gunj. How costly they made our raw material!

The farmer thought for a while. "Are you sure, girl? If the landlords at the Gunj find out, they may be angry—at us for selling directly, and at you for bypassing them."

"These fields are yours, and whatever you grow is yours. The money is mine, and I'm paying you the agreed amount. What's wrong with that? Why should anyone be angry?" I said.

The farmer couple thought for a few moments.

"Please pack five bags of raw mangoes before it gets dark," I added, creating a sense of urgency.

They agreed and packed five bags, charging us fifteen aanas per bag. I happily bid them goodbye and headed back with five bags full of tangy mangoes, a joyous smile from saving fifty aanas, and a surprised look on Anjaneylu's face.

Seeing his expression, I thought, You old illiterate!

When I reached home and narrated the transaction to my mother, she was overjoyed and kissed me on the forehead. She wasn't happy because I had saved money, but because I had started thinking for myself. "Of what use is education, if it can't profit one in some manner," I thought in my heart of hearts.

So, our transactions with the farmer couple continued for a few days—until they caught the eye of a landlord who worked at the Gunj.

Chapter 10: The Grand Act

It was late evening. Darkness everywhere. Someone knocked on our door—again and again. We opened it to find Anjaneylu panting outside.

“What’s the matter?” my mother asked.

“One of the landlord’s sons is coming. He’s bringing some men,” he said.

"Why? So what?"

"Dear, they're coming for Chennamma. They found out about her through the farmers."

"For Chennamma?" My mother's face began to show signs of worry. "What did she do?"

"She started purchasing raw mangoes directly—cutting into the profits of the lords at the Gunj. They want to teach her a lesson."

"Oh my God!" Amma almost collapsed in worry.

I stood silently, not knowing what to do.

"How did they find out?"

"They went to the farmer's house and thrashed him for selling directly. They asked who the buyer was, and he told them it was a girl about their daughter's age—intelligent and charming—someone they couldn't resist selling to."

My mother listened to his explanation silently, like a dead rock.

"The landlords are planning to teach this young, intelligent, and charming girl a lesson. They may abduct her. You need to run away," Anjaneylu warned.

Amma thought for a few moments, then said she would handle the situation and asked him to leave. She told me to go hide behind the grass heap behind our house.

"But what about you, Amma?" I asked.

"Do as I say," she commanded.

I knew that tone. She wouldn't listen to me now.

I ran and hid behind the grass heap, from where I could see the window of our house—and my mother through it. To my eyes, the whole setting looked like a photo frame of someone imprisoned.

In the beginning, I saw the shadows of four to five people enter the house. Under the light of the lit chimney, their grim faces made it clear—they were here to teach a lesson.

As they stepped into the living room, one of them—probably the son of a landlord from the Gunj—shouted, "Hey! Who is Chennamma? Is she here?"

My mother, her long hair loose and flowing over her shoulders, sat on the floor, facing away from them. I shifted slightly, trying to get a clearer view of the scene.

She remained perfectly still, eyes closed, unmoved by the shouts and murmurs of the men who had just entered.

They approached her, puzzled by her silence. The large red bindi on her forehead deepened the gravity of her stern expression. They hesitated to touch her.

One of them grabbed some utensils and threw them to the floor.

"Are you Chennamma, you witch?" one of them barked, finally daring to grab her hair and tilt her face upward toward the ceiling. My heart stopped for a moment, terrified for my mother.

Then she opened her eyes—wide, unblinking, and still silent.

The man shook her head and shouted, “Where is Chennamma? That bloody farmer said she’s beautiful, charming, and intelligent. Let me see her beauty tonight!”

Suddenly, my mother let out a burst of hysterical laughter—“He ha ha!”—and spoke in a loud, eerie tone: “You want to see Chennamma? You want to see Chennamma? Do you even know who Chennamma is?” She laughed again, louder.

The man slapped her. “Stop laughing! Tell me where she is, or we won’t hesitate to harm you!”

Still laughing intermittently, she said, “Do you know who I am?”

“Who are you?”

“I am the mother of Durga. Do you know who Chennamma is?”

“Who is she? A little girl we’ll take away?”

“You fool. She is Durga herself. You cannot touch her. If you ever lay hands on her, you’ll turn to ashes.”

My mother began to tremble violently, as if possessed by the goddess Durga herself.

By now, the man had let go of her. All of them stood frozen, watching her. She was possessed.

“You are mere mortals. Don’t ever think you can mess with the Gods. You cannot disrespect them.”

“What will happen if we do? We just want Chennamma,” one of them said, though his voice had softened.

"You fool. You cannot touch Chennamma. She is a part of me."

"Who are you?"

"I am Durga herself," she said, her body shaking, her eyes rolled back to show only the whites.

"You're not Durga. You're acting!" one of them yelled.

"If you ever lay hands on Chennamma or me, I curse you—you'll rot the very next day and be eaten by maggots. If you touch her, your house will collapse within a week. If you touch her, the farms in this village will burn, and the village will suffer a drought for three consecutive years."

Her convulsions grew more intense.

"But Mother, why should Chennamma buy raw mangoes directly from the farmers?" one of them asked. I could hear the shift in their tone.

"Gods do as they wish. Who are you, mere mortals, to question the actions of the divine? She liked the farmer couple because of their deeds in past lives. She may have paid them more out of compassion. That is her will—the will of the Goddess. Do not question divine acts."

"We won't question, Mother. Please forgive us."

Still in her trance, Mother continued.

"We have one request, Mother. Please ask Chennamma not to buy directly from the farmers. It causes us loss," one of them pleaded, like a son before his mother.

"My son, I am possessed by Durga, and I shall speak only what is right. Whosoever sows, that soever owns. That soever can sell to whomever they wish. You, my son, gather the produce and make it available to the public. You earn a profit—that is fair. But if someone puts in the effort to reach a farmer and makes a fair deal, that too is just in the eyes of the Gods. You cannot call it wrong. Your arrogance in this matter will invite divine wrath. And when the Gods are angry, you shall rot, your house shall collapse, and your village shall suffer drought for three years!"

With that, she closed her eyes and continued her convulsions.

All of them bowed, lying flat on their stomachs before her, and left immediately.

As soon as they were gone, I ran into the house.

Falling to my knees before her, I prayed, "Oh Goddess Durga, please calm down and send my mother back."

She slowly calmed, opened one eye, and asked, "Have they gone?"

I stared at her in silence, feeling a strange mix of awe and betrayal.

"Chennamma, I was really scared. I didn't know what else to do."

"Mother? You weren't possessed? All of this was acting?"

"I didn't know what to do, dear. I just wanted to save you. I had to become possessed for that. I couldn't think of any other way."

"So… you pretended to be a Goddess?" I half-laughed, half-cried, tears rolling uncontrollably down my cheeks.

"Don't cry, my sweetheart. They're gone. We're safe now," she said, holding me close.

"Mother, I'll never purchase anything directly from the farmers again," I said.

She laughed.

I—and that dark evening—were witnesses to the greatest act of my mother. We tried to sleep that night, hearts still racing.

But from that day on, a quiet fear for my safety began to grow in my mother's heart.

Chapter 11: The Wedding Proposal

After her grand act, my mother didn't send me anywhere for the next few days—not even to school. Occasionally, one or two neighbors dropped by, who by now had become good friends of hers, thanks to her pickle business. It was during these conversations that the first ideas of my marriage began to take shape.

My mother rarely shared much about our lives, but in those days, she expressed her fear openly—especially when she recalled how those men had asked her, horrifically, *"Where is Chennamma? That bloody farmer said she is beautiful, charming, and intelligent. Let me see her beauty tonight."*

I remember exactly when it began. One fine evening, my mother and our neighbor Kalpana aunty were sitting on the veranda. As the sun was setting, casting a dim golden hue over the day, my mother said, "After that evening's incident, I worry a lot about Chennamma. I don't know what to do next for her safety."

Kalpana aunty, who was almost the same age as my mother, listened quietly. She took a long breath, as if to add weight to her words, and said, "I think it's time... I think it's time to get Chennamma married. She's thirteen already—and she's hit puberty too."

My mother remained silent for a few moments, gazing at the sun, which had nearly disappeared, leaving behind the last fragments of light. Then she turned her head and looked at me. I was pretending to work in the kitchen, but I was listening to every word.

"Maybe... maybe it's time," she murmured. "A girl's mother always prepares herself for this sort of thing—the marriage of her daughter, to send her off someday."

I knew in that moment that my mother had made up her mind. And that thought felt even more terrifying than the incident with the landlords.

"But where do we find good boys these days? And who would want to marry a girl with no father or brother?" my mother asked Kalpana aunty.

"Oh dear Rukku, you've forgotten the old saying—if we search, we can even find the invisible God. We'll find a son-in-law for you in no time, especially when the little bride is beautiful and her mother runs a thriving pickle business in a small village," Kalpana aunty said, fuelling my mother's determination further.

I felt like murdering her then and there.

***

After Kalpana aunty left, I sat with my mother. I knew she was up to something—I always recognized that look on her face.

"What's it now?" I asked.

She smiled but didn't say anything.

"Tell me," I insisted.

"Hmm... let's find a nice boy and get you married," she said. She wasn't exactly smiling, but she tried to stretch her lips into something that resembled happiness.

"Mother, do you remember when I was around four, and you once told me that I should marry and take care of my man?"

"I don't quite remember," she said, lines folding across her forehead.

"You're lying. What did I say when you told me that?"

"What did you say?"

"I said I wouldn't marry or go anywhere. If I marry and take care of my man, when will I take care of you, my sweet mother? I don't want to marry and leave you—or this place."

Small droplets of tears welled up in her eyes. They rolled down, just like the last time we had this conversation.

"But my little one, it's a custom, a rule. A girl has to get married eventually and stay with her husband."

"Mother, who made this rule? We should find that person and beat the hell out of him," I said.

Mother smiled. "I don't know who made it. Maybe society did."

"What is society?"

"A group of people living together."

"How can society make such a rule? It clearly favours boys. Why can't a boy leave his house and come stay with a girl's family?"

"Boys who do that exist—but they're very rare. With our connections, I don't think we'll ever find a son-in-law willing to stay with the girl's family. And even if we did, society mocks such boys, calling them unmanly," my mother mused.

"First of all, what is the need for marriage? We're living so happily—why can't we just live like this forever? Why, Ma?"

"Child, today I'll answer every question you have. You deserve clarity about this decision," she said, making me sit beside her on the floor under the window. "So your question is: what is the need for marriage, right?"

"Right," I said.

"I don't know the exact answer, but I'll share my understanding with you. There are multiple reasons why one gets married."

"Multiple reasons like?"

"Hmm... the first reason is safety. See, I'm thinking about your marriage because of last night's incident. Since you're young and beautiful, some men may try to take advantage of you—prey on your slightest mistake or rebellious act. If you had a husband, that risk would be a little less," she said.

"You're trying to convince me, but if I had a husband in your place last night, he would've been dead by now."

Ma didn't laugh at my joke. She continued.

"The second reason we marry is for happiness. Once someone feels safe and protected, they feel happy too."

"I don't understand what you mean, Ma. Were you happy after marrying my father?"

My mother sighed. Then she said, "I was happy after you were born."

"Was father a good man?" I asked.

She remained silent for a few moments.

"How was your married life? Tell me."

"It started off with a huge promise—a promise that was never fulfilled. So, I'd say my marriage was… okay," she said.

"When you weren't happy being married, how can you think I'll be happy? Isn't that wrong thinking, Mother?"

She smiled. "Just because one flower in the garden wasn't good doesn't mean all the flowers are bad. Similarly, just because one person wasn't good doesn't mean everyone in the world is bad. Think positively, my child. If all the people in the world were bad, it would be better to wrap yourself in a blanket and sleep forever. But there are good people too. Remember the lady who offered us her golden bangle? Remember Anjaneylu, who warned us in time and helped us escape the landlord's goons?"

I remained silent for a few moments.

Then I asked again, "Amma, it's still not clear to me why one should marry."

"Child, I already told you—it's for safety, happiness, and the continuation of life."

"Then why is it only the girl who must leave her house and go live in the boy's house? Why can't a boy come live with the girl's family?"

"Those are rules created by society, my child. And it's better not to question them."

"But Mother, the new person... I'll never know if he's good or bad. And on top of that, I'll have to leave you. I can't leave you. I just can't, Mother. Please," I pleaded.

"My dear child, don't be afraid. I won't be able to look after you forever. You'll have to take care of yourself—and in this society, you can't live alone. You need a partner. I promise I'll find a good boy for you, and you'll be happily married. Is that okay?"

I didn't say anything. I could feel that my mother was completely sure about what she was doing.

The evening finally turned into night, and there were no more words between us—just as we cannot see anything in the dark, there was nothing more left to say.

***

The next day, my mother sent out a message that we were looking for a groom.

But unlike what she had expected, no one turned up. It wasn't an easy task. Some said, "Who will marry a fatherless child?" Others added, "Who will marry a girl who doesn't have a brother? Who will help us out in the future? And we'll have to take care of her mother in her old age—we can't do that."

Oh! How cruelly people think, I said to myself. Secretly, I was happy that no one was interested in me. But my mother grew more frustrated with each passing day.

In the meantime, I was enjoying school. I had learned how to read. My teacher used to say, "Those who can read a word slowly begin to read the world." It was fascinating to see thoughts take shape on paper. I loved reading stories and news, and I had fun with my friends at school.

Some more months passed like this.

One fine day, a matchmaker visited our house with unexpected news. My mother looked at him with hopeful eyes. He sat on our veranda, accepted a glass of water from her, and then broke the news.

"There is one party interested in your daughter. Just like you are mother and daughter, they are mother and son."

"How old is the boy?" my mother asked.

"He's just 22—very suitable for your daughter."

"What does he do for a living?"

"He's a landlord. He employs others on his farm and collects the harvest," the matchmaker replied.

My mother remained silent for a few moments.

"Why would a landlord be interested in my daughter?" she asked.

"Oh dear, your daughter has become a little famous. The landlord heard about her through others at the Gunj. He listened to how people praised her beauty and brains. Since then, he's only thought of your daughter."

My mother didn't respond.

"From the moment he learned you were looking for a match, he's been hellbent on marrying her. He told his mother he'll marry only Chennamma and no one else. Finally, the mother agreed and sent me to speak with you," the matchmaker said.

My mother's stern face slowly lit up with a smile.

"Are they good people? Will they take good care of my daughter?" she asked, her voice full of hope.

The matchmaker gave her a look that seemed to say, 'What are you even asking?'

"There are just the two of them, and they live in a beautiful house atop a hill, surrounded by trees and birds. They'll take good care of your daughter."

"Oh, if this is true, then what more could I want? I'll send my daughter—a piece of my heart—happily to their home. Please ask them to visit us and meet our beautiful Chennamma," my mother finally said the words I had feared most.

The matchmaker left, assuring us he would return soon with the mother-son duo.

I wasn't happy with my mother's plans, so I pretended not to speak to her. When she came and stood near me, I turned away. When she called my name, I buried my face in the book I was trying to read. I ignored her as if she were my enemy.

After some time, frustrated, she held both my shoulders and asked, "What is it? Why are you behaving like this? Do you think I'll be happy sending you away?"

Her eyes filled with tears, but her broken words continued. “This has to be done. It’s for your safety and happiness.”

I stood silent for a while, unable to bear her tears.

“Ma, please don’t cry,” I finally turned toward her.

“If you want me to marry, I will marry. Let them come tomorrow. Let’s meet them first,” I said.

“And don’t marry just because I’m saying you have to. You should agree with confidence—with the belief that your marriage will be strong,” my mother said.

“Okay, Mother. I’ll do that. I’m just afraid of leaving you, that’s all,” I said, clutching her tightly as my eyes welled up.

It was the first time I saw my mother cry—and it was heartbreaking. Maybe one of the saddest things in life is watching our Gods fall.

***

Finally, the mother-son duo arrived at our home.

He was twenty-two. Looked alright. Tall and polite, with a voice like sweet payasam—just a little too sweet. His mother wore gold up to her elbows, but her smiles looked fake; they never reached her eyes.

“Chennamma is such a pretty name,” my would-be mother-in-law said.

“It means brave,” my mother added.

“Ah, how sweet. But beauty suits a girl more than bravery,” she said, smiling at me.

I smiled back, sitting uncomfortably in front of two strangers.

“So, let me get to the point directly,” she said, looking at her son. “This is my son Prakash.” Then, shifting her gaze to me, she continued, “From the time he heard about your daughter, he’s been saying that if he were to marry, it would only be a girl like Chennamma.”

“And what does the son’s mother think of her son’s desire?” my mother asked, as I served them water.

“I’ll be happy if my son is happy. That’s why I’m here,” she replied.

“What about the son’s father?”

“He died a few years ago due to cholera,” said the son—my would-be husband.

“And the girl’s father?”

“He passed away in his sleep due to health issues, some years ago,” my mother said.

“Though we are in a far better position than you, I assure you we’ll take good care of your daughter.”

“I know it may not suit me to ask, but I will anyway—since the girl’s father isn’t alive. May we know about the son’s property?” my mother asked hesitantly.

“It’s perfectly fine to ask about the place where you’re sending your daughter. I understand,” said my would-be mother-in-law.

"He owns twenty acres of land. We grow mango trees, paddy, and watermelons," she added.

My mother remained silent, listening.

"Do you have anything else to ask? Please go ahead," the woman offered.

"What do you expect from us in this marriage? I don't have anything except my daughter—who is my heart—and some pickles," my mother said.

"You should give something, just for the sake of society," the woman replied.

"But I don't have anything else," my mother said softly.

"This house. Why don't you give this house?" the woman asked, glancing around.

"This house? I'm sorry. But where will I stay if I give it away? Where will my daughter return to visit me after marriage? We can't give it," my mother said in a pleading tone.

Confused, I looked at my mother. And the man hadn't taken his eyes off the saree-clad me.

"Oh, that's also right," the woman added. "You should have a shelter. I was joking. Why not give away that barren acre of land? It's yours, isn't it?"

"Yes, that's mine. But what will you do with it? It's just a useless patch of land," my mother said, even more puzzled.

"It's alright. My son often conducts experiments on barren land to convert it into fertile soil. This will work, won't it?" she asked.

"Yes, I can give that as dowry for my daughter and son-in-law," my mother said.

"Then it's settled. Let's find an auspicious date and make them husband and wife," the woman said.

"Yes," my mother replied with a smile.

"Here's to our happy times—let me sweeten your mouth," she said, opening the box they had brought.

She took out a saree and placed it on my lap, then fed me a laddu. A mini celebration of new beginnings, I thought.

My mother just watched us, tears silently rolling down her cheeks.

In that moment, I realized I didn't belong to my mother anymore—I wasn't her heart, and she wasn't my body. We were two separate individuals, meant to live our own lives.

The overly smiling son and his fake-smiling mother finally left. They left behind a silence—a heavy, suffocating silence between me and my mother—after announcing the marriage date for the following week.

***

That silence lingered for two or three days. Then one day, my mother stood face to face with me and asked, "Chennamma? Won't you talk to your mother?"

I turned away in anger and stepped out of the house. I paced back and forth in the front yard, then marched toward our barren land. I looked at the trees, the birds, the sinking sun. The question circled in my mind—Why should I leave my mother for the sake of the world?

I kept walking, eyes shifting between the black soil and the blue sky. Then I heard a soft "Moo..." from a cow being milked. I stood there, watching the fresh milk flow from the cow's bosom.

And somehow, in that moment, I understood what my mother was trying to do. I had purchased that cow with the ring my mother had once bought for me.

I brought Nandini—the new cow—into our house.

"Chennamma, what are you doing?" my mother asked, arms crossed.

"Amma, this is Nandini. I bought her for you. She'll keep you strong after I go. You have to drink her milk every day and take good care of her, okay?" I instructed.

My mother burst into tears.

"Amma, don't cry. I understand you. I will not only marry—I'll take good care of myself and my man," I said.

She hugged me tightly.

"...and my mother-in-law too. They seem like good people," I added.

The remaining days passed with the three of us—me, my mother, and Nandini—enjoying our time together. And then came the final night before my marriage.

The house was decorated. Everything had been washed. The walls were whitewashed. Flowers filled every corner they could find, adding their beauty to our little home.

And I lay there, my head resting in my mother's lap—my eternal protector.

"What have our lives been until tonight?" I asked.

"A beautiful chapter of a mother and daughter's love," my mother replied.

"What does tomorrow signify?"

"A hopeful new beginning."

"What if they're not what they seem?"

"Then I will look into them."

"Are you sure, Amma?"

"No," she said, her voice brittle as a cracked mirror. "But sometimes, we have to walk into the fire before we know if it will burn or bless."

Silence settled between us.

"Ma, how did my father die?" I asked, though I already knew the truth.

"He died because of his bad karma," she answered dryly.

What felt like a few moments of peaceful sleep in my mother's lap turned the night quickly into a new day—the day that would change our lives forever.

***

Amidst the chants of sacred vows, a few smiles, and a few sad moments, I got married to Prakash—my husband.

After the ceremony was over, I finally bid farewell to my mother, my house, and my everything.

As I sat on the tanga, watching it all drift away through tear-filled eyes, my husband's voice tried to reassure me: "Everything will be okay."

I closed my eyes and felt the weight of growing up. And I understood—growing up carries a heavy weight.

When I opened my eyes, I found myself in a new world. The tanga was climbing a hill, toward a solitary house. I called it the house on the hill. And in that dark hour, it looked ominous.

Chapter 12: The Deceitful Treasure Hunt

This—where we are right now—is that house, the house on the hill.

I woke up to a new morning, and the ominousness of the house seemed to fade.

My husband came into my room. "Good morning, is everything okay?"

I smiled and said, "Yes. Good morning."

"Get up and get ready, Mother has cooked breakfast. Let's have it," he said.

"Okay, I'll be there in a few moments."

He just left. He didn't sit beside me, didn't play with my hair. I thought, maybe I was expecting too much, too fast. What my friends had told me about the first night and the following days wasn't happening as quickly as they imagined. How would they even know? They weren't married either, I thought.

I got up, dressed, and went to the hall where we were supposed to eat.

Mother and son, who had been talking, suddenly stopped when I entered.

"Chennamma, come. Sit down with my son," said my mother-in-law as I stepped into the living room.

I didn't say anything. I sat beside my husband. My mother-in-law served us food. For a moment, she reminded me of my own mother.

Everything felt dreamlike.

"Chennamma, I used to do all these household chores till now, but you should start taking them over after some days. Is that okay?"

"Okay, Mother-in-law. I will do them," I said.

"Chennamma, my mother and I are going out to buy some tools for farming. You stay at home and take care of it," said my husband.

"Sure. I will," I replied.

After eating, they left, leaving me alone in this new place. I wished we had those cool gadgets back then—I could have called my mother, maybe even seen her face. Since I didn't, I just lay down, relaxed, and imagined her in my head. She must be missing me terribly, her eyes red because I was gone. Or maybe she was busy taking care of Nandini. Perhaps Nandini was calling her "Moo!"—just like I sometimes called her Ma.

Then, I took a brief stroll through the house, examining it.

The kitchen, the living room, bedrooms, verandah, front yard, backyard, an opening to terrace from inside—everything looked fine, but still there was something mysterious about this house.

Up the steps, there was a small storeroom. Inside were tools I had never seen before, and maps I couldn't understand. I tried to read the words but struggled. The map had villages, terrains, and water bodies marked. I even located my house on it—a small dot. What alarmed me was that it had a red dot on it. I didn't know what it meant, but I wanted to find out soon. Maybe they were just noting all their properties. I went back to rest.

Since the mother and son had told me they'd return in the evening, I thought it would be better to cook for them. I chopped vegetables, made curry and rice, and waited.

They arrived just before evening. As they walked in, I heard faint words carried by the wind: "She will never know about it." Who was that "she"? Me?

They fell silent once they entered the house.

We ate together. It felt like a good time. Later, we returned to our rooms. My husband and I were finally in one room. I was afraid, shy, and wordless. But there was nothing much to fear or be shy about—because he only talked and talked. He spoke about his mother and how much he loved her. He spoke about the market they had visited. Then he said he was tired and went to sleep.

I thought, maybe it will take time for him to listen to me, to get closer to me.

I also fell asleep.

When I woke up, the same pattern continued for the next few days—except they no longer went to the market. Instead, they discussed things behind closed doors. Something suspicious.

One day, my husband said, "You must be missing your mother. Let's go to her place."

I was overjoyed, and the three of us set off immediately. We reached my mother's home within a few hours.

The joy of seeing my mother knew no bounds. I screamed with delight at the sight of her, "Amma, I am back!" as I entered the front yard of our house.

Her face lit up with a big smile upon seeing me.

"Thank you for coming," she said to all of us.

"You should also get to see your daughter sometimes," my mother-in-law added.

For a moment, I felt extremely grateful toward her.

We had lunch together, though with some awkward silences here and there. Then the mother and son said they wanted to look at their one-acre barren land. "We would like to check out our land. My son has planned some experiments to conduct there. We'll go and come back," they said before leaving.

I was finally alone with my mother. At last, I had time to talk about everything under the sun.

"So?" my mother asked.
"So what?" I shot back.
"How is everything? Are you happy there?"
"It's fine, Amma. They seem to be good people."
"Does he love you? Take care of you well?"

"He is good. He talks a lot—mostly about himself and his mother," I said, hesitant to speak about the distance between us.
"Will you have children soon?"
That was a question I didn't expect.
"Woah, slow down, Amma! I just got married two weeks ago."
"So what? I was just checking."
"Looks like someone's in a hurry to become a grandmother."
My mother chuckled.
"You have changed," she said.
"No, I haven't."
"You're cracking jokes just like your mother-in-law."
I laughed it off.
"Ma, I want to ask something."
"Ask."
"Is it common for a newlywed couple to maintain distance in their initial days?"
"Distance? As in?" she asked.
"Distance that I cannot talk clearly about with you."
"Hmm... sometimes it may take time. You have to..." she paused, then continued, "you have to dress up well, cook good food, become a great friend, and slowly the distance may fade."
I nodded. I was shy talking about these things with my mother, but I remembered her advice: good food, dressing up elegantly, becoming a good friend.

We both watched the mother-son duo from the window. They looked like tiny insects searching for food in the barren land, talking continuously and restlessly. They were inspecting every inch of the land they had received in dowry.
"What are they looking for in that barren land?" I asked.
"I don't know."

"Doesn't it look suspicious?" I pressed.
My mother stayed quiet for a few moments.
"There's nothing suspicious. They said they want to conduct experiments on barren land, so they may be examining it thoroughly," she finally said.
I nodded, agreeing with her.
Then I told her about my new house, how I was slowly settling down there, and a few things about the mother-son duo. My mother just listened. *Maybe listening is loving,* I thought.

The familiar picklish aroma of my mother's house, and Nandini's "Moo," finally made me feel lively again. At my husband's place, I often felt imaginary—but here, I felt real.

Finally, they returned.

As they sat in the living room, my mother-in-law said, "We would like to come here often, as my son wants to dig and excavate this land for his experiments. He wants to see if it can be turned fertile again."
"Sure. That sounds like a great experiment. You can come here anytime," my mother replied.
I was happy, knowing I would get many chances to meet her again.

And so, the excavation began.

Most of the time, my new family—that is, the three of us—lived in my mother's house, especially when these experiments were being conducted. My mother-in-law and husband were deeply absorbed in their work on the barren land. They toiled tirelessly. We didn't quite understand their approach, nor how they intended to turn this barren land into fertile soil. Yet they excavated every inch of it, as though it were some secret experiment. At times, even my mother and I were not allowed near.

Sometimes they returned with tired faces, and sometimes with dissatisfied ones. But eventually, I grew accustomed to their all kinds of faces.

In my new house, my responsibilities were to take care of the home, cook for my new family, and look after my husband – my man. He always boasted about his mother and kept a certain distance from me. I didn't understand the reason for his behavior. But we simply carried on—until one day.

One day, my husband returned home with a red face and a newspaper in his hand. He jolted the door hard while entering, making a loud sound. I asked him, "What's the matter? Why are you so angry?"

He shot an outrageous look at me with his sharp, frightening eyes. He went in and shouted, "Amma, see this," laying the newspaper in front of his mother.

"What happened?" she asked.

"Look here, this headline. The hidden treasure of Nizam finally unearthed in the village of Kusumapura."

"What? Really?" my mother-in-law asked.

"Yes. It is the same treasure we've been searching for. We are deceived, Mother."

My mother-in-law was speechless for a few seconds.

Her son grew restless with each passing moment. His steps marched back and forth, his hands brushing through his hair, clutching his head. Suddenly, he sat down and cried loudly like a child. "Maa, we have lost it. We have lost it."

"Don't cry, my baby. It's okay," my mother-in-law tried to pacify him.

Witnessing all this and realizing the truth about their activities was shocking for me. I didn't know how to handle the situation. The angry, grieving mother-son duo terrified me. But I gathered courage and sat in front of my husband.

"Hey, it's okay. Look at me. We have each other," I said softly.

He looked at me for a few moments, then suddenly began swearing.

"You bitch. It's because of you that we're in this situation."

"What?!" I was stunned, unable to respond.

"I should have married the girl from that farmland where the treasure was found."

"What? Do you even know if the people who own that farmland have a daughter to marry?" I asked, my blood boiling.

"How dare you talk to me like that? You bitch!" he shouted, slapping me hard. I almost fell to the ground.

That was the first time I was beaten. I got up and sat on the floor, tears rolling down my face.

"Yes, son. She has brought bad luck to us," my mother-in-law added.

"Was it not you who came to our house saying you had heard about me?" I sobbed. "Didn't you say your son only wanted to marry me and no one else?"

My mother-in-law gave me a deceitful look.

"See how she talks to elders. How dare you? Is this what your mother taught you?" she said venomously.

"How dare you talk to my mother like that?" my husband shouted, slapping me again.

I stopped crying, stood up, and quickly went into my room to pack my things. Soon, I saw their shadows behind me.

"What are you doing?" my husband asked.

"I'm leaving for my mother's home. I cannot stay here another second," I said.

"You cannot leave us. I married you. You are my responsibility."

"I don't care. You beat me. I'm leaving."

My husband grew furious again.

"How dare you talk to me like that?" He hit me hard, and when I tried to get up, he kicked me back down. He grabbed the bag I was packing and threw it far away.

"One more word out of your mouth, and I'll kill you." He locked the door from outside.

I couldn't believe this was happening. One evening, one news article, and the real colors of the mother and son were revealed.

Then came the days of torture. Locked inside the room, I was deprived of food and water for two days. After continuous pleading, the door was finally opened—the door to the harsh reality of my world. I was no longer the sweet, loving wife or daughter-in-law. I was just an object of criticism. Their words hit me like relentless waves:

"You are good for nothing."

"Have you ever seen your face in the mirror? What did my son see in a dark pig like you?"

"You are as infertile as the acre of barren land given in your dowry."

"Both mother and daughter are cunning. See how they trapped us with nothing."

"You can't even mop floors, cook properly, or wash clothes and dishes. You are truly good for nothing."

I had never been treated this way—not even by my father, who once wanted to kill me at birth. I believe he wouldn't have treated me like this if my mother had been there. Oh, how I missed her in those days. Tears rolled down my cheeks when no one was watching, because even crying was forbidden. I yearned for my mother desperately. Only she could rescue me from this abyss.

One day, she came to our house.

I was taken to a separate room and warned not to speak of anything happening at home, or the consequences would be dire. I had to obey.

Now, the criticisms were directed at my mother:

"How can you come so frequently? What will people think?"

"The barren land you gave in dowry is as barren as your daughter. She couldn't produce anything."

"Hey, you dark, ugly woman, serve water to your mother."

Naturally, my mother was shocked, stunned, and speechless. They revealed everything they hadn't wanted me to say. She looked at me, and I knew she sensed the horrifying problems I was facing. Which mother can bear to see her child treated this way? I felt her blood boil that day. I knew she would return to rescue me. But for then, she left, apologizing for the hardships the mother-son duo claimed to endure because of my supposed bad luck.

My miserable life continued. Real misery is felt when one is not respected, not given a place to belong, not heard, beaten into silence, and ignored as though dead while still alive. That is true misery.

One day, my mother visited again. The mother-son duo shot angry looks at her. She apologized for her sudden arrival and explained her purpose.

"I met a spiritual guru with magical powers. He visited our village recently, and I was lucky to be at the temple that day. I told him about Chennamma's infertility problem. He smiled and gave me this medicine, which looks like a temple offering. It must be consumed by the husband before consummation to yield offspring. He told me to give it to you along with ten grams of gold."

She handed over both the gold and the offering, then left. She didn't even see me. She didn't ask the reason for my supposed infertility. I had never even been given the chance to consummate my marriage.

A few days later, my husband finally touched the gold. Then he inspected the offering. He was always a suspicious man. He took it outside. I thought he was foolish enough to believe that eating an offering without being with me would grant us a child. But he wasn't that foolish. He whistled, and a dog came running. He fed the offering to the dog and waited. Within two minutes, the dog died.

I was stunned. My mother had planned this – this unexpected thing. My mind totally stopped working. The world spun around me, the floor pulled out from under my feet. I didn't know what consequences this attempt would bring.

Soon, two policemen visited our house. They saw the dead dog and inspected the offering my mother had given. My husband spoke:

"My mother-in-law is a dangerous killer. The rumors were true—she might have killed her husband too. See how she planned to murder me. Even her daughter would have died if she had eaten it. The motive is simple: she doesn't want to hand over her property to me. And since we have no children, she thought we were useless. So, she decided to kill me. Please jail her and take strict action against her for planning to murder an innocent man."

And soon, my Amma was put in jail.

I didn't know what to do. The only thing I kept telling myself was, "Why did Amma do this?" My heart sometimes answered that question. Maybe she felt bad seeing me treated this way. Maybe she was enduring the same pain of separation as I was. Maybe she wanted to keep me happy by destroying these monsters who would never let me be free.

Amid all this turmoil inside me, I wondered—what next? What should I do now? I realized that the only God I could pray to was my husband. I fell at his feet like a broken, withered flower and made desperate appeals for him not to harm my mother. "She must have received the offering directly from the guru. She cannot hatch such dangerous plans. Please don't do anything to her. I will do whatever you say. I will live like a slave for you forever. Please. Please. Please."

But the heart of my man did not melt. Yet one fine day, by God's grace, he agreed to release my mother from jail and not pursue the case further—on one condition: that we both would never meet again. I knew that never meeting her was equal to death, but at least she would live. That was enough for me. I agreed.

And finally, I took a long, peaceful breath once she was free in the open air. I knew I could never meet her again, but I was happy to imagine her freedom in my thoughts.

Chapter 13: Letters To My Mother

For a long time, I didn't meet my mother. I suppose I will never meet her again. Since we could no longer see each other, I resorted to a new way of communicating with her. I knew she couldn't read, but I also knew she would find a way. So, I secretly wrote my first letter to my Amma

—----------------

My dear Amma,

I am very happy to know that you are out of jail. I have always loved the little things you did for me—the effort you took to send me to school by traveling so far, always cooking delicious food for me, and trying to lift my mood during the most frustrating situations. I truly appreciate everything you did.

And trying to kill my husband? Ah! That was a bombshell, a mind-blowing thing you did. I can't imagine the courage it must have taken. I really wish he —------

Love you, Amma,

Your Chennamma forever.

—----------------

When the mother-son duo weren't at home, I climbed down our little hill and dropped the card into the post box near the next village. I also befriended the postman who was approaching the box and asked him to deliver the letter to my home only when my MIL and husband were not around. I felt he understood my situation and agreed to my request.

I waited for days for the postman's arrival. I desperately longed to read some words from my mother. I waited like the night waits for the day. As more days passed, my hope of receiving a reply slowly faded. The heart that had blossomed with hope was now withering. The waiting was painful—like a shard of glass piercing through my skin.

I waited under the vast blue sky, which made me feel the tiniest and loneliest. I waited beneath the green trees whose leaves were turning yellow and shedding, reminding me to let go of my memories of her. And then, one day, when my husband and MIL were not at home, the *tring-tring* of the postman's cycle reached my ears. I rushed out of the house like a torrential river.

"There is a letter for you, little one," the old postman said.

"Oh yes, it is for me!" I cried, snatching the letter from his hands and running inside.

I came out once more and shouted, "Thank you!"

I saw the postman smiling as he trod down the hill in the sunset.

I eagerly uncovered the letter and read it.

—-----------------

My dear Chennamma,

You cannot imagine how happy I am to receive your words. They have breathed new life into me. I never imagined that a simple piece of paper and pen could help us talk. How have you been, my little one? There are so many things to share, but I am still figuring out how to put them down on paper.

Your loving Amma

—----------------

And from that day onwards, our letters flowed like the endless current of a river. But it was a secret river known only to my mother and me. We stopped addressing each other as Amma and Chennu—a silent understanding that even if our letters were intercepted, we would be caught. We even created code words for safety, danger, and fear. "The sun is shining today" meant we were alive and well. "The cow is hungry again" meant I was mistreated. "The grain is rotting in the sack" meant danger was lurking nearby.

—----------------

"While going down the hill to post the letter, I saw a woman. She walked just like you. For a moment, I thought it was you. My heart almost leapt out of my chest—until she turned around. I may have forgotten your voice, but never your silence. How is Nandini?"

—----------------

"Sometimes, when I dream, I see you as a baby again. I feel like I should have kept you in my arms and never let anyone touch you. I tried to give you wings, but they were burnt. I am sorry. Nandini? It has grown so much—it is now about to deliver a baby. And how about you, my sweetheart? Are you onto anything special?"

—-----------------

"Today, the sun is shining. I swept the floors and saw a peacock through the window. I hummed a song to myself. For five minutes, I forgot I was a prisoner—I simply existed. It felt strange, yet warm. I'm not into anything special. Sometimes the cow is hungry. I think you remember that."

—-----------------

"Oh, that was so bad of me to ask. Your letters made me feel as though you were right beside me, happy. Do not worry, sweetheart. In a few days, the sun will not just shine—it will shine its brightest. Do not worry."

—-----------------

I knew my mother was a fighter. I wished I had the same spirit in me. Since I didn't, I waited for my hero to arrive. She hatched a plan—to give a bounty to a gang of thugs who would come to my place and secretly bring me to her. The planned night finally arrived.

I was waiting like a princess kidnapped and locked in a witch's chamber. The gang came at last. With turbans on their heads and faces masked, they crept in quietly. They hushed me from my room to the outer hall, and finally, I was outside. Soon, I was on a horse tanga, descending the hill, inching closer to my mother with every second. Though fear gripped my heart, excitement surged at the thought of meeting her.

"But wait, this is not the way to my mother's house," I shouted at the tanga rider. He looked at me, said nothing, and turned his head back to the road. I realized then—I was drifting away from everything.

Next Morning.

The sun did not shine brightly; clouds shrouded it. Crows cawed over a banyan tree where the village heads sat. I stood before them—hair messy, face tear-streaked, barefoot, bruised not from violence but from betrayal. My husband and mother-in-law stood as silent victims. A crowd had gathered—neighbours, old women, children, judgmental aunties, whispering men. Silence hung heavy.

One of the village heads began sternly: "We haven't gathered here for judgment, but for clarity. Chennamma, Prakash's wife, was found escaping from her husband's house like a thief in the night. What do you have to say, Prakash?"

My husband replied in a slow, sad tone: "I gave her everything—food, shelter, respect. But she still tried to leave without telling anyone. As there are no signs of beatings or bruises, it is clear she left on her own. Why should she leave if she has no reason?"

My mother-in-law added, "She dishonored our house. My son treated her like gold, but she spat in his face. What kind of mother sends thugs in the name of rescue? That woman—Rukmini—is cursed. Poisoner of men, now thief of daughters!"

People muttered: "Today's girls are oversensitive. One slap and they leave the house." "She should have discussed it with elders before taking such a step." "Maybe she tried, maybe they didn't listen."

I understood then—I was the only one who could speak for myself. “Do you call that place a home where you are not allowed to talk to your own mother? What kind of home is that?”

“Oh dear! You can always meet your mother. You just have to take permission from your husband,” said one village head.

“My husband won’t give it to me,” I whispered, almost in tears.

“Prakash, why won’t you give her permission to meet her mother?”

“Sir, the entire village knows the story. Her mother tried to poison and kill me. And if the rumors are true, she murdered her husband too. Why should I send her to her mother? They will conspire to kill me,” said my husband.

“Why don’t you leave me then? Let me live my life on my own,” my conscience cried out.

“First you try to kill my son, and now you defame our family in broad daylight. Enough of this sympathy! She must be disciplined before every girl in the village thinks rebellion is a virtue!” shouted my mother-in-law.

“Yes. The girl’s actions were inappropriate. She is going against her husband’s wishes. After marriage, your husband is your everything. What will you do after your mother passes away? Who will take care of you?”

“I will work like my mother. I will take care of myself,” I explained.

But my words were ignored, dismissed with looks of contempt.

"Since no harm was done, let her remain in her husband's home. She will not contact Rukmini again. That woman has already tasted the law. If Chennamma tries anything again, she will be sent to her father's ashes, not her mother's hut."

I wasn't ready to step back into that house—that haunted house on the hill where there was no love, no hope, no life. But my husband and mother-in-law dragged me back like an animal.

The sun did not shine at all. The cow was very hungry. The grain totally rotted in the sack.

Chapter 14: Regressive Thinking Of My MIL and Husband

After this humiliation came darker days I hadn't imagined even in my worst nightmares. My husband and MIL made plans to tie me to them forever. The plan was chillingly simple—get a baby out of me.

What followed was a nightmare I wouldn't wish on anyone. My husband's approach to sex was unimaginable and unbearable. He would drink, get completely intoxicated, walk to me, hit me, and then invariably rape me. Again and again.

The worst kind of punishment is being forced into sex with someone you utterly loathe.

During those horrific times, I would whisper to myself, "Bear it, my heart. Just bear it. It will be over soon."

Months passed. Nothing happened. There wasn't a sign of a child inside me. "You are indeed as barren as the piece of land given by your mother. You are good for nothing," my husband would shout.

Amidst all those dark moments, I longed to reach out to my mother—just one more time. This time I wanted to write more secretly. But the moment I tried to put my pen on paper, there was the tring-tring of the postman's cycle. I ran out to meet God's messenger. I snatched the letter from him. He would never know how grateful I was. This slowing heartbeat needed a reason to keep beating a little longer—and that reason was the letter.

I opened it.

—-----------------

Dear Chennu,

I'm writing this with trembling fingers, not because of fear—but because I imagined never being able to call you mine again.
I was told never to speak to you. But silence cannot stop a mother's voice. Even when I was locked in that cell, I tried to talk to you, wishing that the wind would carry my words to you and yours back to me.
Are they feeding you properly? Are you safe? Do they hurt you?
If you see a hibiscus bloom outside your window, know that it's the same as the one I planted near our doorstep. We are still connected by root and blood.
Keep your head high, but your voice quiet—for now.

With love that cannot be chained,
Amma
—-----------------

Amma,

The hibiscus outside my window bloomed yesterday. Red as sindoor, but softer than all the cruelty around me.
I am safe in the way a bird is safe inside a cage. I'm not beaten, but I am being unmade—one stitch at a time. I smile when they speak. I bow when they glance. I cook. I clean. I exist.

Your letter smelled of turmeric and old tears. I kept it under my pillow. It gave me the strength to look into their eyes and not blink.
Sometimes, when I make rice, I add a clove—not for them, but for you. So your name tastes sweeter in my thoughts.
Tell me about your garden. Do the marigolds still grow?

Yours in silence,
Chennu
—-----------------

My dear heart,
Children are like flowers that bloom in the garden of life of parents. How can a parent be ever happy when their flowers are mistreated?
Oh yes! The marigolds have bloomed like fire in our garden. I speak to them when I miss your voice. They don't answer, but they nod when the wind blows, and I imagine it's you, replying softly.
The village says I'm a curse, that I poisoned my husband, and now a son and a marriage. But what they'll never understand is that I was never trying to kill anyone—I was only trying to save you.
Some lives are gardens. Ours is a battlefield.
But you, Chennu—you are the sword they couldn't see hidden in my sari.
Stay still. But sharpen quietly.

Your mother,
Who never surrendered
—-----------------

Amma,

Today the mother-in-law called me a ghost in her house. I smiled. If only she knew how right she was.
I have stopped crying. Not because I don't want to—but because the tears have grown tired.
I talk to your hibiscus every morning. I whispered a secret to it yesterday: "One day, I'll leave not with tears, but with thunder."
Do you still sing when you grind the rice? I try to hum your tune, but I think I am forgetting it.

Your daughter,
Who has become flame inside clay

—-----------------

My Chennu,

I dreamed of you yesterday—not as a bride, or prisoner, or daughter—but as fire. Walking, not burning.
My bones have grown quiet. My breath has begun to slow. The doctor says I need rest.
But how does a mother rest when her daughter lives in chains?
If I don't write again, know this: You are more than a victim of their greed. You are more than the daughter of a jailed woman. You are the wind after fire. You are what remains.
If you ever leave that house, do not look back. Let the world burn behind you.
I go now to rest under the hibiscus tree. If the wind rustles its leaves, it is me, brushing your cheek.

With every heartbeat left in me,
Amma
—----------------

Amma,

I waited by the hibiscus today. It didn't bloom. It just stood there, still and silent. Just like me.

They didn't let me come. They said you were gone. That I had no right to cry. But I did. I cried into my hands. Into the kitchen rice pot. Into the folded cloth where your last letter hides.

I will not let your fire die. One day, Amma, they will know your name. Not as a prisoner, but as a mother who birthed a flame.

I am still here. But not for long.

Your fire,
Chennamma

—-----------------

And that was it—the end of my Amma. I never received another letter. My lifeline had come to an end. I existed like any other rock on this planet.

The world around me didn't change. It remained the same vicious one. The guilt of not being able to sit at the feet of my dead mother and pray for her, the guilt of not being able to sprinkle her ashes in the flowing river, the guilt of not being able to fight back, of not being able to be like her—a fighter—ate me bit by bit every day.

My mother was gone. Now it was the turn of my father. Lifeless. Hopeless. He possessed me. I just existed as he did. My father's gifted the mindset of fear as a heritage to me. Now, with no one in the world who was mine, I trembled at the slightest rise in the tones of my MIL and husband.

The gossip of the mother-son duo grew louder each day. I paid no attention. They would stop as soon as I stepped into the room, exchanging glances as if wondering whether I had overheard. “Go to hell with your gossip. Go to hell with your exchanged glances,” I would say to myself.

Chapter 16: My End and Stranger's End?

It was just another lifeless day where I had to feed myself simply to stay alive. Why should I even stay alive? Why do people live—for someone, for something, or just to live?

I didn't have someone to live for. I didn't have something to live for. I simply didn't want to live. But it was one of the promises I had made to my mother—that I would live to the best of my ability until age itself took me away. That I would not do anything foolish to myself, because I was the apple of her eye. She was watching me every second, from the twinkling of the stars to the rustling of the leaves. I had to fulfil that promise of staying alive.

Even my personality was undergoing a drastic change. With my mother, my courage died. And fear resurrected. Fear was my father who always thought that a girl would be a burden forever. I was a burden to my mother till she passed. Was he right?

These thoughts made me weak and fearful. These thoughts made me reclusive of my own company. Spoken words were less. Obedience became fullest. Slavery was the mantra to survive.

One day, I was eating while the two devils of my life gossiped about something. I filled my stomach and soon felt dizzy. As I stood up, the world around me spun at lightspeed, and the earth beneath me seemed to vanish. I collapsed. I struggled to breathe, suffering with excruciating pain in my abdomen. I cried out in agony, sweating all over. I cried for some time until I finally lost consciousness.

I was unconscious for some time. When I opened my eyes, I found myself tied to a chair with shackles—helpless. My hair hung loose, sticking to my sweaty face. My frail body trembled, and my eyes were swollen from whatever had been mixed into the food.

Once a familiar room now appeared dark and damp. Cracks ran like veins along the faded walls. A single weak bulb swayed from the ceiling, casting crooked shadows. The air smelled of kerosene, sweat, and dust. Broken furniture lay scattered like skeletons of a forgotten past. An old barrel stood like a silent witness.

I saw those two people standing near me. My husband — tall, lean, with sharp features and hollow, unforgiving eyes. The other was my mother-in-law — a short, stout woman with a permanent sourness carved into her wrinkled face.

I asked weakly, "Why did you tie me like this? What harm have I done to you?"

"What did you bring us? What did you bring us?" the mother-in-law repeated, her voice spilling venom. "Ever since you stepped into our house, we have faced only losses. No prosperity. No children. No good luck," she said bitterly.

"How am I responsible for that?" I cried helplessly for a while and continued, "I have cared for you from the day I left my mother behind — the day you snatched me away from my own family. You didn't even allow me to meet her. I couldn't even attend her funeral. What more could I have done for you? What do you want from me now? Please, I beg you."

Husband answered coldly, his voice like a blade, “We don’t need you or your services anymore. You are of no use to us. You came to us with nothing — just a piece of barren land — barren like you!” he shouted.

The mother-in-law sneered, “Now, my son has a proposal from a wealthy family. They promised us lands and gold. And then...”

I pleaded, “You want to marry again? I accept it. Let me stay. I will live like a servant. I will take care of everyone. Please, just set me free.”

The mother-in-law’s voice was sharp. “No. We didn’t tell them my son was already married. If they find out, we lose everything.”

“Then let me go. Far away. I will disappear from your lives. You’ll never hear from me again. Please, set me free.”

“That’s not possible,” said my husband, his eyes gleaming with greed. “We cannot take chances. There's too much at stake.”

Greed danced in their eyes, wild and ugly.

“So what are you going to do?” I whispered.

“We are going to get rid of you,” he said simply.

My heart raced. “Get rid of me?... Get rid of me? What do you mean?”

‘Get rid of me’ seemed familiar. My father always wanted to get rid of me as he thought I was a burden to his life. Now, my husband and MIL were also thinking the same.

He said, “Huh, I’ll show you what getting rid of someone means.” He opened the barrel and poured its contents over me. The choking stench of kerosene filled the air. I felt it soak my skin, my clothes, and my soul.

I screamed at them, “Please don’t do this! I have done nothing but serve you! Everyday — cooking, cleaning, caring — everything for you! What harm have I done? Please — please, have mercy!”

I cried. I cried. And I cried.

But they didn’t listen.

Finally, the mother-in-law lit a matchstick, her wrinkled hand steady with cruel purpose. Her face lit up with greed in the glow of the matchstick’s flame.

“What is my mistake in all of this?” I sobbed.

“You are a woman,” the mother-in-law said.

My voice broke, “Hmm...Aren’t you a woman too?”

The mother-in-law’s lips curled into a cruel smile. “I am different. I have a son.”

“Please — please don’t do this to me!”

But no one listened.

They dropped the burning matchstick on me.

I burst into flames. I screamed — a sound so raw, it could have torn through stone. Through the flames, I saw the idols I had always prayed to, every morning and every night. I thought Gods will come and save the good people. But Gods never came to save me. I couldn't tell whether it was I who was melting, or if it was the idols burning in the fire.

And then, I stopped screaming.

I sat silent — like a blackened statue.

The man and his mother exchanged confused glances. Why wasn't I screaming anymore? Even as the fire devoured me?

There was silence. A total silence except the sound the ruffling fire.

And then — A massive explosion. The fire roared up like a furious beast, tearing through the walls, shaking the earth, and splitting the very sky apart.

And then, there was darkness everywhere.

The house on the hill remained standing for decades afterward. Silent. Watching. Waiting. No one dared to come inside. No one knew what had truly happened here. It simply stood — a haunted house on the hill.

So, I died. But I didn't ever move out of this house but I sent my husband and mother-in-law to the Gods. I really enjoyed killing them in the fire of my fury. I ensured that nothing of them was left, not even the ashes.

And now it's your turn as a stranger. I lifted him holding his neck and threw him down on the floor. The stranger was doomed to die in my hands. I brought the knife and kept it on his neck and looked at his face for one last time.

PART THREE

Chapter 17: Stranger made me feel good after a long time

Just as I was about to slit his throat open, I saw that he was crying rivers. He was not crying out of pain and neither was he crying in the fear of death. He was crying just like I did during my lonely days and nights.

His stupid gadget kept asking, "Boss, are you okay?" at least ten times "I can hear that you are crying. I hope the ghost..argh..Chennamma is not being harsh to you."

His eyes had gone red and lips a little twitched. I didn't feel like killing this guy. That thought vanished from my mind like some magic. I threw the knife aside with a clanking sound. He got up and brushed his hair back, cleaned his face with both his hands like a young child does after crying and sat back on the chair as if he wasn't at all beaten. Poor guy!

Facing the radio, he spoke something which I had always wanted to hear but no one ever spoke to me.

"You know Chennamma. You have gone through so much. I can only imagine the pain you must have felt all along your life."

"Maybe even after my death," I added.

He smiled lightly with his sad face and continued. "Your father wanted to kill you on your very first day. Your mother fought to save you right from the same first day. No doubt, you are sometimes so weak that even a petal's fall on the ground could scare you, and sometimes, you are so strong that you carry the energy of a thousand stars in you."

"I can only imagine the times you come from," he said, thinking.

"Times have not changed much even now. Do you remember the sack in which a young girl was brought? Raped, beaten, and almost killed?" I added.

He gave an assuring nod. "I agree that the times have not changed much even now. But education is slowly changing the ways of how people live. People used to live like passing clouds without any conscious thoughts. Now, slowly, consciousness is taking over the souls that have lived in the dark for a long time."

"I don't think so," I added "I hate God for creating an unjust world. His world favours men over women, strong over weak, cunning over innocent, evil over good. I just hate God and his world."

"Chennamma, I can understand what is making you say that. Your father tried to kill you on your first day by drowning in water. What a horrible thing to even imagine? Then, he constantly looked for ways to let go of you from his life. He even tried to sell you away when you were a small child. I can only imagine the wounds his actions might have inflicted to your soul right from your childhood." He broke into tears saying this.

I never imagined that one could be so sensitive towards another's suffering. For the first time I felt my hands missing. I would have patted his back and said "It's okay dear" like my mother used to do to me. I really missed my hands.

"Hey stranger... Aarav. It's okay. Do not cry." He recomposed himself. He was silent for a few moments.

To break the awkward silence, I spoke, "You said you were hungry just before I bet you and told my story. Are you still hungry?"

"Yes, I am hungry as hell."

"Oh, let me cook for you. You are my guest in this haunted house." I tried to lift the pan on the floor and the noodle's packet near his bag pack. I tried multiple times but I couldn't do those simple things. Maybe I was just dealing in killing for so long that I forgot common household chores.

"Let me help you," he lifted those things and walked near his small portable stove.

It was a beautiful sight to watch him cook his food. The last person I loved watching physically was the post man who delivered my mother's letters. There was a sort of kindness in their eyes, a sort of understanding of the turbulence in my mind.

He finished cooking, then sat on his chair again facing the radio and began eating. I enjoyed watching him eat his food. I hadn't been able to see him clearly all this time because of my rage. He was a lovely man in his thirties, crying even at this age. He had long, thick hair that covered his neck completely and his shoulders partially, kind eyes, and lips as pink as roses. His nose and chin weren't as sharp as my husband's; they were slightly rounded at the corners, yet looked elegant as they carried no trace of cunningness.

The air again felt heavy with the awkward silence between us. So, I started.

“So, do you always go like this? Is this your job?”

“Umm. Yes,” he said while gulping down his food.

“So, you talk to ghosts like me quite often?”

“Nope. This is my first assignment.”

He finished eating his food and drinking the water. I felt relieved at his hunger getting satiated. He ate like he hadn’t eaten in ages.

“So, are you getting paid to imprison ghosts?”

“Yes. sort of.”

“Are you going to imprison me?”

“I don’t know.”

“Even after listening to my entire story?”

He was silent. Then he spoke in a thoughtful tone again looking at the radio. He didn’t know I was looking at him through all angles.

“You were just saying that you hate God with your complete heart because he created an unjust world. Do you remember that?”

"Umm.. Yes. I do remember. And I stand by my words. I hate God."

"Would you be open minded to listen to something I want to say so that you would feel good and relieved?"

I was getting very relieved today. First by telling my story, then by letting him eat. And now, he wants to make me feel even more relieved by saying something very nice. What a day!

"I am all ears," I said.

"You know that people say that not even an ant moves a step forward without God's permission. Have you heard that saying?"

"Yes, I have heard it. And that's the reason I hate God. He gives permissions for all sorts of things: good, bad, ugly, and the ugliest!" I shouted back.

"But that saying is wrong. Not even an ant can move a step forward without God's permission is wrong."

"What?" I asked doubtfully.

He gave a pause almost lost in himself while talking. And then resumed.

"If there is God, an absolute God who is the most beautiful and the most intelligent and the wisest, then he will not give permission for all sorts of things like the good, bad, ugly and the ugliest. With his permission, only flowers bloom, only new lives spring, only rainbows come, only stars shine, and only good thoughts and feelings emerge from hearts and minds of the human beings."

“Then what about me? I was about to get killed on my very first day of life. Where was God at that time? Where was God when I was burnt alive on the last day of my life?” I asked furiously.

“I will say that God wasn’t there to help you. But I wouldn’t say that God got you killed.”

“Then, who killed me?”

“Let me explain again from the beginning. If there is God, an absolute God who is the most beautiful and the most intelligent and the wisest, then he will not give permission for all sorts of things like the good, bad, ugly and the ugliest. With his permission, only flowers bloom, only new lives spring, only rainbows come, only stars shine, and only good thoughts and feelings emerge from hearts and minds of human beings.

Then who does the evil deeds? These are done by the beings who got disconnected from God. More precisely, they are done by human beings who have lost touch of this supreme force and are living an ignorant life.”

I was silent. I didn’t want to interrupt him. He continued.

“All human beings are necessarily not evil beings. Most of them are still in touch with God. How? God is a manifestation of assimilation of all the good in the world. This manifestation is exhibited by most of the human beings in everyday life. For example, your mother, wasn’t she the Goddess who was there to protect you from the day one of your life? She herself became the God who came to save you when she started kicking her husband even though she was suffering with the worst of the pains of a new mother. She eventually killed her husband to protect you. Then, she did all the brave things to give you a great life. Ah! How she became a beggar for you? How she became a business woman for you? How beautifully she tried to get you educated when most of the world was still in slumber and ignorant about women's education. Your travels in disguise, your little adventures of deceiving people like beggars, your mother's ultimate action like a possessed Goddess to save you from the wrath of landlords, most importantly the everyday love and care showered upon you by your mother – these things no matter how many times you recollect, you will cherish them as eternally beautiful memories. Your mother is a manifestation of God – the manifestation of all the goodness in the world."

I was lost listening about my mother from someone else for the first time. How beautifully this stranger was describing my life spent under the warm wings of my mother. I missed my eyes to shed a few tears in her memory. I really missed the human body. But the beautiful memories didn't stay for long, because there came the word 'but'.

"But," the stranger continued.

I felt like the good things had come to an end.

"But, your mother wasn't as perfect as God. She was very near to that Godliness but she lacked certain things. The ability to make right decisions."

"Stop! One more word about my mother and you will be dead," I gave a warning on a very serious note.

"Chennamma," his soft voice kind of assuaged me, "you wanted to tell me your story rather than getting caught in a bottle. I listened to you. But do you know that you are already caught? You are caught eternally in this haunted house, a place where your mother doesn't exist. Let me help you be free."

Some moments of silence ensued.

"It's just that I can't hear anything wrong about my mother. She is my only God," I said.

"I understand and feel your pain. But sometimes, only bitter medicine can cure us."

Had I had my physical form I would have closed both my ears with my hands and permitted him to talk. Since I didn't have those hands, I let the stranger say those bitter things about my mother, "continue."

"Your mother was a brilliant human being—a brave heart! But she wasn't as perfect as God. She was very near to that godliness, yet she lacked certain things, like the ability to make the right decisions. While we glorify the purity and beauty of Gods, we often fail to understand the intelligence of God. A God who does nothing evil and only does good is truly the most intelligent entity in this universe. We are all descendants of Gods, and as soon as we lose touch with God, we become ordinary people. Without proper day-to-day education, we make poor decisions and end up in bad situations."

"What did my mother do wrong? She always wanted a great life for me," I said.

"Yes, she always wanted a great life for you, and that's why she wanted to educate you. She sent you to a teacher. Your intelligence was growing, and that education was giving you the power to question. You questioned the society framed by powerful human beings who may or may not have been in touch with God. Your simple question was, 'Why can't I directly purchase the fruits from a farmer?' Wow! I truly admired your courage—and you even purchased them directly. It enraged those powerful landlords, but your mother's spontaneous act averted the situation. You were saved, once again."

"Then?"

"But this incident left a serious impression on her mind—an impression that sowed the seed of fear for your future. She worried for you, and worry is not a great emotion. It makes us take all sorts of poor decisions. As suggested by her friend, she immediately started to look for the right match for you, without even letting your education be completed. This was the only poor decision taken by your mother," he explained and paused.

"What would have happened if I were educated? Wasn't I supposed to be married and take care of my man anyway?" I shot back at him, who said that my mother had made the wrong decision.

"One way of looking at life is seeing it as a dangerous jungle. You don't know which animal will pounce on you if you are living in a state of slumber. Education is the weapon to protect yourself. It will give your tiny wings the power to fly in an unending sky, and it will make your fins so strong that you can swim the deepest waters. Education will give you sound logical reasoning that will help you make the right decisions at the right time. Your mother truly wanted to provide that kind of education to you, but fear for your safety slowly dominated because of your conflict with the landlords."

"One silly mistake of directly purchasing fruits from the farmer cost me my life. How terrible was the thinking of landlords who thought of attacking me, a young girl! I am certain they were educated. But they behaved like animals. What's the point of education, then?" I asked furiously.

"Yes, they were educated, but they still remained like animals. That's because the education imparted to them couldn't instill one of the key elements required for a great life—emotional thinking. Now, they had the power to fly wherever they wanted. I know they were wrong and you hate them. But you must admit that they attained skills which helped in their independence. They were stronger than many others, just as lions are stronger than deer in a jungle."

"You call those idiots lions? They were cunning foxes, afraid that a girl would start a revolution by buying goods directly from the farmers. The farmers were suffering too," I debated, totally engrossed in the conversation.

He smiled. "Ok, let's call them foxes—but they were still stronger than the deer."

"Excuse me. So you are calling me and my mother deer?"

"No. Your mother was a ferocious lion, a brave heart. She could go to any extent to save you, but sometimes even lions make mistakes because of the fear of society."

"By society, are you referring to the landlords?"

"I am referring to that segment of society who are powerful and cunning, and who have lost touch with God—the assimilation of all good things, everywhere, every second. Why should we be afraid of a society that's good?"

"Sounds logical. But you are calling me a deer, then? How did I end up such a pussycat while growing under the wings of a ferocious lion?"

"That's because of your father."

"Oh! He looked so dangerous to me. I was always pulled towards him as a child, but with a huge fear in my mind. He tried to sell me away in the market."

"What kind of parent only wants a boy child? An uneducated parent, whose mind is filled with fear and who thinks females are far inferior to males. Those kinds of parents do many dangerous things. When this fear snatches away their logical reasoning, they commit the evilest acts, like..." He was about to finish the sentence, but I completed it.

"Like killing a baby on the first day of her life?" I snatched the words from his mouth.

"Yes. Like killing a girl child on the first day of life. Like treating a girl as a burden to carry. Like treating a girl as an open treasure whose life is always in danger, as anyone can come and steal it. Like blaming a girl for every flood and famine. An uneducated parent has a sick mentality. There is no logic left in their heads. Your father was mentally sick."

"Yes, I always dreaded him. But aren't all men like that? Aren't they all mentally sick?" I continued, "I clearly remember the story of Poornamma, my father's friend's daughter, who committed suicide as she was getting married to an old man. I clearly remember this when my father explained to my mother why a girl child is a problem. As a child, I was also convinced that he was right. So I think that all men—and some women—are already mentally sick because of the fear associated with a girl child. You are a man. What do you think?"

"I don't believe in that. I believe that everyone is born equal. Everyone has the ability to think and develop intelligence, and eventually incline towards God—all the goodness in the universe. And I also believe that education can develop this ability. Education can cure this sickness because it will let common sense prevail. Common sense, put simply, is the right use of mind and heart. Common sense will whisper to you that just because thousands of people are doing it, something wrong doesn't become right. And it also whispers to you that just because one person is doing it, something right doesn't become wrong. Similarly, a good thing doesn't become a bad thing, and a bad thing doesn't become a good thing. Education is the ability to discern and choose exactly this: right from wrong, and good from bad."

"Sounds fair. So where did my father go wrong?" I asked.

He adjusted himself on the chair, thinking for a moment while looking at the ceiling. Then he inclined towards the radio and spoke. "He is a classic example of a typical man who has been listening to society, and mind you, society will shout loudly with its purpose—that one has to eventually lose common sense and believe only what it is trying to dictate. In your father's case, society was shouting this: A girl child is a curse, a burden, and a bad investment. Society convinced him so much that he totally believed it and was ready to kill his daughter on the very first day of her life."

"How could society get that power to snatch his common sense away?"

"Often, it is the powerful who set society's thinking in motion. And who are considered powerful? The rich, the landlords, the politicians. What they do is copied by others. Imagine: I am a wealthy man with a daughter and a son. The moment my daughter comes of age, I think of marriage. If I give her equal rights, I must share my property equally between my son and my daughter. But my daughter will leave for another man's home, and if I give her an equal share, that another man, my son-in-law will become rich. *Oh no!* Why should I make another man rich? Better to give her something as dowry and be rid of her. *Oh no!* I have a daughter, and when she grows up, I must part with my property as dowry and send her away. She is a liability. Better God had not given her to me!

This is precisely how a person in power thinks—and in doing so, becomes a vicious role model for society. There is no logic in it. Who is this "other man"? The daughter's husband, who will have his own progeny. Yet to justify their thinking, the powerful claim that a woman cannot aid in the progression of her father's race. But what of the son, who marries another man's daughter and has children? How can he alone be called the progressor of his father's race? It is utterly illogical, far removed from God—the goodness that exists everywhere, all the time.

And the common man, looking up to these role models, begins to follow their rules: *I must do what the powerful man does, to be what he is.* Unknowing that the powerful man is as drowned in troubles as he himself is. Where there is no education, there is illusion. And where there is illusion, there is confusion."

"That's too deep," I interrupted, "so you say that my father was a victim of poor societal thinking. I get it. Then, what's education? I really doubt our society will ever get educated."

"Education is one knock on the brain's door to wake up from deep sleep and think clearly, and one beautiful tickling on the heart to rekindle and feel dearly, to express those feelings in words. Most of the people will get educated at some point in time because life itself is the best teacher. And some will never get educated till they die, as they won't get any opportunities and as they have no will power to get education in their lifetime."

"Like that of my father? My husband? And my MIL?" I intervened.

"Yes. And even you, who have been on a rampage of killing people."

I kept silent for a few moments. Silence felt awkward, and words needed to fill the air.

"I didn't kill good people. I killed the bad. They were rapists, vulgar living beings," I justified my doings.

"I know they were bad people, but all bad people are victims. Yes, they need punishments for their offences, but that's only the human view of seeing it. It is not God's way, not a divine one," he said in the sweetest voice so far.

I was compelled to ask, "Then, what's God's way of dealing with these bastards?"

"A good God will never punish sinners; there is no hell in his world, as he loves everyone equally. Then, naturally, the only other option is that he will replace hell with an education system that makes them realise the horrible web of negative things in which they are stuck."

"Then, what's true education?" I asked.

"Ability to think rationally on our own to deal with the situations of life," he answered effortlessly.

"Why did God create us?"

"Think of God as the roots of a great tree—the mother. Everything else is born from those roots. The main trunk of this vast tree is society and the living world, and we are like its leaves—parts of God sent here to enjoy this beautiful adventure of life. Like God, we too are limitless.

The purpose of our time here is to enjoy and cherish life by nourishing ourselves with good thoughts and good actions, so the great trunk remains strong. By being good and doing what is right, we eventually find our way back to God."

"Then, why do people fight with each other? Kill each other?"

"It is simply because they are ignorant of the concept that we are all part of one being. That's why when you hurt someone, you yourself also feel disturbed—because you have harmed yourself too in that process. When you make someone happy, you make yourself happy too. People are ignorant of this basic fact. People are also ignorant that living with ethics is the fundamental quality for being happy. They treat others as aliens and do strange things that push them further into ignorance."

"What about my husband and mother-in-law? The star actors?"

"They have copied the quality of loving fake wealth from the leaders of the herd. First, let's understand true wealth. Having a loving soul around you in thick and thin, and being a loving soul for that wonderful being—that's true wealth. Your mother and you were two such wonderful souls. Next true wealth is taking care of the beautiful nature, which gives us things to nourish day in and day out. Understanding the true power of our inner selves and finally merging with the universal power—that's true wealth. The people who fall in love with fake wealth take another way. They love gold, money, houses, and strange things. They are totally ignorant of true wealth. They are so ignorant that they can even do vicious things to get fake wealth. There is much more they suffer with."

"Like?"

"They cannot express themselves clearly. The ability to express one's feelings in simple words is a mark of emotional maturity. Instead of speaking out when they feel angry, they throw things, beat others, and even kill. Instead of expressing their happiness, they cut themselves off from others, thinking they are superior. Instead of expressing their sorrow, they mislabel the emotion as hatred, blaming someone for it. So, first they love fake wealth, and then they suffer from a lack of emotional maturity. That's the opposite of progress—regression. Regressive thinkers go back; they don't use the divine organ, the brain, to understand the world, to connect with people, to connect with nature, to connect with the supreme. Instead, they feel like they are a single entity, and everything should come and attach to them. They don't understand that God is all beings. Your husband is a classic example of a regressive thinker. No doubt he married you for the mysterious treasure rather than marrying you for love and enjoying your company."

"What's a marriage?"

"It's a sweet promise between two people to live and share this beautiful journey of life together," he said in a sweet voice. He looked even more beautiful from the way he was expressing things. I was impressed head to toe, though I didn't have any of them.

"What about my mother-in-law?"

"A mother-in-law is someone who becomes a mother to a new child because of the law of society. She has to first become your friend. But your mother-in-law never became your friend. She simply copied her own mother-in-law, who must have tortured her, and she must have seen others doing it. And she simply exhibited the same behaviour. She was a poor, uneducated soul."

"And a killer too," I added.

"Poor, uneducated souls finally become a threat to the very living. Regressive thinking slowly changes into self-destructive thinking, posing a threat to other lives as well."

"Where did my mother and I go wrong?"

He paused and breathed deeply. He was thinking.

"The moment your mother was afraid of the landlords and thought of marrying you off was the first place where you went wrong. Choosing the wrong life partner was the second mistake. Agreeing to their every silly demand is wrong. It is not wrong to say no to silly demands from anyone in life. Why should you leave your mother after marriage? Why couldn't the boy come and live with you?"

"Because his mother would become all alone."

"Then, what about your mother?"

"Who cares about a girl's mother? That's the way society—your society—is designed," I shouted at the poor soul.

"That's where you are copying society and not thinking on your own. You are agreeing to the rules of society ignorantly."

"What should I have done?"

"You shouldn't have married a person who was not ready to live with your family, while you were ready to leave for his family."

"Oh dear, I would never have gotten any marriage proposal in that case," I kind of laughed at his silly explanation.

"What's the point in marrying the wrong person? Isn't it better to live a happy single life than fighting the devils each day?"

"But hey, think about how society will talk about me—males of all age groups shooting glances at me. This is what my mother was worried about all the time, wasn't she?"

"Okay, everyone will shoot glances at you. So what? I know you were afraid of them because you were weak."

"Yes, what would have happened to me after my mother passed away? I would not have lived without her any longer," I retorted.

"You are copying society again and not using your own brain. Who told you that you are weak? Who created a mental picture of a weak woman in your mind? Why is it so hard for you to imagine a stronger self?"

I was silent for a moment at his indignant explanations. "Where do these weak pictures come from?" I asked.

"Like I said already, the powerful are the role models for society. The powerful want to control the women in their homes by painting gentle and weaker pictures of them so that they can be chained to kitchens, babysitting, household work, and kept away from rightful property shares and strong education. These powerful people think of wives as slaves to the home and daughters as liabilities who will not even aid in the progression of their race. They forget that we are all of God's race. They think that their son, who marries another man's daughter and has a child, progresses their race, while their daughter, married to another man's son and having a child, cannot progress their race. They live in a very fake illusion. And society takes them as role models just because they have lots of money—which isn't even true wealth. And you have copied pictures set by those powerful fake notions."

"Then, how should we have pictured ourselves? How should my mother have pictured me?"

"Imagine yourself as strong as your mother. What hasn't she done for you? She saved you on your very first day, kicking your father away even while enduring the agony of labour pains. She did countless beautiful things to care for you. She became a beggar, a businesswoman, and a caretaker. She killed your monster father, and she would have even killed your husband if it meant saving you. She was strong, fierce, and brave—yet loving, rational, and tender.

Picture her: a woman who walked barefoot on burning roads, yet carried you in her arms with unshakable devotion. A woman who bent her back to earn a coin, yet stood tall like a lioness when danger approached. A woman whose tears watered your dreams, and whose laughter lit your darkest nights. She was a storm when she had to fight, and a gentle breeze when she had to heal.

Imagine. It is not hard to imagine yourself receiving education daily. It is not hard to imagine having a strong body that can protect itself. It is not hard to imagine having your own herd where no harm can step in. You should have pictured yourself as a strong, clever lady with an even stronger circle of close companions. You could have pictured yourself as a powerful businesswoman, just as your mother was striving to become. You would have become one of the powerful in society—someone other women could model themselves after and emulate."

Again, had I had a physical body, my eyes would have cried rivers when he addressed about my mother. How was I so blind? I could have become like my mother and would have never left her side. I would have married someone whom I trusted, someone who could have returned all the silly things I did for him. Even if I didn't find such a match, I would have found some lovely team, we could have flourished my mother's business. Why were we not using our common sense and simply copying society? I understood what the stranger wanted to say. Life is simple if we use our brain and stop copying others. I understood what he wanted to convey. Then, one question still remained.

"What about me now? Was I wrong to kill all the bad people?" I asked.

"Harmful acts are ways of displaying our anger when we are not emotionally mature -- when we are not able to convey that anger in the form of words. You were denied a shoulder to lean on and express all the sad things done to you for a long time. At one point, the atrocities against you were very bad, and you were denied the chance to talk about them completely, ultimately leading that regression to become so strong that it created a monster out of you who has been justifying her thoughts. Yes, they were bad people. Extremely bad people. And you took matters into your hands because these people somehow exhibited the characteristics of those terrible ones you had encountered in life. But that is not the purpose of life."

"What should I have done?"

"You should understand everyone—how they achieved their criminal mindsets, how they are stuck in a vicious mental web that causes so many social atrocities. You should understand that they are only the superficial layers of a complex problem. Just killing them won't solve the problem. You cannot solve a problem without working on the roots: poor societal thinking. No matter how many such criminals you kill, new ones will come, on and on. Hence, what you did didn't matter much in solving the problem. It is not your battle to fight with them. You have already avenged the sinners of your life. And now, it is no longer your place to be here and take care of the world—just forgive them, evolve, and go to a better place."

"What is that better place?"

"The better place is like the lap of your mother. In the better place, you will feel the same as you felt in your mother's presence. In fact, this universe is everyone's mother. You have to take a step to let go of this harmful anger which kept you stuck in this haunted house on the hill by embracing eternal power. You are not here to be bound in a haunted house; you are here to dissolve back into the universe where your inner peace lies. It is a beautiful thing."

I smiled at his explanation. "Isn't every house that treats girls so badly like this haunted house on the hill?" I asked.

He reflected my smile on his lips. “Yes, every house that treats girls—or for that matter any other human being—in an ignorant way, degrading their morale all the time, is a haunted house on the hill. I agree,” he said.

“Let me think for some time. What you said is too much for me to process,” I said. I thought about everything: my beautiful little house in our village, my hero mother and all the beautiful things she did for me, the disguises and gambles, the small school where I went to study, the farmer from whom I purchased raw mangoes directly for a business bypassing landlords, my mother taking on the role of the possessed one, then getting married due to fear of the future, then my MIL and husband, the bad people being deceived due to poor planning in their conspiracy, then ultimately blaming me for all their incompetencies, then my mother planning to kill them to save me but ultimately getting caught and jailed, then my husband releasing her on terms that I wouldn’t ever talk to her, then the secret letters between my mother and me, then my plan to run away from home but getting caught, and society demanding me to stay back with my husband, then my mother’s death, then the marital rape episodes, and ultimately being killed for not bringing enough for them. I was burnt alive. But I didn’t die because of my anger towards God—I just stayed here, engulfing those bad people in my rage of fire. I enjoyed my stay here as a ghost in this haunted house on the hill. I enjoyed scaring people, even killing some bad ones, then rejoiced looking at their devices, thinking this was it. I would have lived like this forever had a stranger with curly hair and his stupid bot not come here. I tried to scare him, even kill him, but he was so powerful that he could imprison me in a small bottle where I would have just been idle like a mad thought. But when I asked him, he listened to me, lent me his ear. And oh boy! How curious he was while listening to my story. He gave his complete attention to me, like my mother used to give. He didn't just listen—he cried for me. I missed my hands after a very long time. I actually wanted to pat him on his shoulder and say, "Hey, it's okay. Come on, stop it, dear." He was a stranger but still understood me so much, felt so much of what I felt. Then, he tried to make me understand where I was going wrong, like my teacher. He is a beautiful soul who might have come here finally to light up the lamp in my kitchen which had not been lit for a long time. Yes, there are bad people in the world. But they are byproducts of complex problems going on in society. Killing them won't actually solve the complete problem. But I have had my share of revenge on society, and now, it is time to think clearly. For a moment, I thought of this stranger as one god who came to stop a goddess who had taken the avatar of a devil and gone on a killing spree. She killed so many people that she wasn't getting satiated. But this god came under my feet and took away all the negativity out of me. He somewhat appeared like that God to me. So now, a beautiful world is waiting outside this haunted house to embrace me in its beauty. I feel like my mother is waiting outside for me. I have to return to that loving place. I was finally thinking clearly."

All the while, the stranger—so confident about his work—was packing his luggage. In the heart of his heart, he knew that I was alright and that I would move out from here. He had the power to understand me. He packed his things and stood up with his talking bot in his shirt pocket.

"So?" I said.
"So...?" he said.
"It's time to move. It's time to return to the lovely universe. I think my mother is waiting there," I said.
"Yes. It's time for you to find peace," he said. "How do I know that you are gone?"
"Just turn off this radio and I will be on my way," I said.
"So, it is a goodbye?" he asked.
"Yes, it's a goodbye," I said.
"Goodbye, Chennamma." His voice was the sweetest after my mother's.
"Goodbye, stranger," I said.

He turned off the radio. He stood there for a few moments, watching it. All the windows of the house finally opened, letting the light enter. The doors were wide open, the fresh air of the morning slowly filling the house. New rays of sunshine made the house look golden, and I felt like I was shattering into a million pieces and dissolving into nature. It was a happy feeling.

The stranger turned around and walked away from the radio. "You have done quite a job, boss," said Tom, his bot. He chuckled like a hero and slowly walked out of the main door of the house. He was now completely outside. He turned around to have a glimpse of the whole house.

"Hey Tom, finally the haunted house has lost its eerie aura and looks radiant," said Aarav, the stranger.

"I cannot see it, boss. But from your voice, I can feel that you are proud of your achievement," Tom responded.

I just gazed at them. They walked and walked. Now they were taking a turn to get down from the hill. For some time, he looked like the postman who had brought my mother's letters. He occasionally stopped at some plants, appreciating the beauty of their flowers. How could I see so far from the house? I think my horizon was expanding. I was not limited to the haunted house anymore. It was a great feeling but, wait! Somehow, I couldn't expand further. My ideas just stopped at the stranger. I felt like I had some unfinished business with him. And maybe that unfinished business was love—I was not sure.

Chapter 18: It's time to go but something's missing

What was I thinking? A ghost or an evil spirit who had just been enlightened to live a larger life was falling for the guy who helped her get out of her mental rut. Oh, I felt so guilty, but my superpowers stayed limited, not interested in any big things. I was lost in my reverie. What power do the light of a thousand splendid suns hold in front of a stupid feeling like love?

As I was thinking, the stranger, who was now halfway down the hill, turned around to look at me—the haunted house. Amidst the flowery bushes, he sat on a big rock, looking at me, thinking about something. The clouds over his head moved swiftly and made way for new light to fall over his face, making him look even more handsome. If someone from far away looked at us, they might see us like two lovers gazing at each other during their meeting of a lifetime. Only, my body was in the form of a house—a confused one who just yearned for some more time with him.

And then something unexpected happened. He was walking back towards me. My heart, though I didn't have one, started to beat faster. I didn't know what to do. I felt like a betrayer who had betrayed a promise made to a good man. I was happy that he was coming back, and I was scared that he would be hurt and I would be the reason for hurting him. I was even more scared to reveal that I was in love with him. But nothing could save me now. He approached me and stepped into my body, standing right inside my heart—the very place where I was burnt alive. Now, my heart was burning with love. Why had he come back? Was he also feeling the same? My stupid thoughts kept going on and on.

"Boss, I could sense the same atmosphere from where we left. Where are we?" Tom asked.
"We are in the same house. I somehow feel like Chennamma is still here. She hasn't left this place," he said, examining the place with his sceptical eyes.
He kept his belongings down and placed Tom on the same table where he had been kept previously. He called out, "Chennamma, are you still there? Can you hear me?"
I didn't respond. I was afraid. Scared.
"I know that you haven't left this place yet. Why? Why are you still here? You promised me that you would leave," he shouted, looking at the walls and various rooms of the house.
All I could respond with was silence.
"I know how to make you speak, you betrayer," he shouted in anger.

I thought he would take the mini bottle outside to capture me again. But no—instead, he took a robe out of his bag. I didn't know what he was going to do with it. He shouted my name for some more time, and then suddenly curled the robe around his neck and started to squeeze. He was strangling himself. I desperately wanted to stop him, but I was not able to find a medium to communicate. This guy was going crazy, and I was searching for a way. In a few moments, I found my electronic impulses and connected to the radio, moving it up and down to gain his attention. Breathless as he was, he finally saw the radio.

He stopped his suicidal act and moved towards me in the same breathless fashion, turning on the radio.

"Have you gone mad?" I shouted at him.

He was still regaining his breath.

"What was that? What were you thinking?" I continued angrily.

"So, you haven't left yet?" he asked.

"Leave about me. What was that you were doing?" I threw my anger at him.

"Listen to me."

"No, I won't. I didn't expect this from you," I shouted.

"Listen to me, please. I know breath control. I can stay breathless for three minutes. I just wanted to bring you back to communicate with me," he said.

"You may have a hundred magical powers, but that's not the way to make me talk. I was so worried about you and wasn't able to figure out a way to communicate with you," I said.

"I am sorry, but we are here now, back to talking," he said, sitting in the same chair.

Silence filled the atmosphere for some moments. He broke it with his sweet voice.

"What happened, Chennamma? Why couldn't you leave? I thought we understood and believed each other," he said.

"Hmm. I don't know what's stopping me. I want to go out and unite with nature. I really want to, but I don't know what's stopping me," I said, hiding my love towards him.

"There is nothing that our mind doesn't know. Just try to express what's stopping you, and we will figure out a solution," he said, sounding like the problem solver for every problem.

If I had a head, I would have scratched it a hundred times to say something else apart from my love for him. I was a bit lost.

"Chennamma, are you there?" he said, waking me up from my thoughts.

"Yes, I am there. I don't know what it is. Maybe I would like to talk with you for some more time," I said in my best natural electronic tone.

He leaned forward, smiled. "Tell me, what do you want to talk about?" he asked.

"Hmm, you know almost everything about me. And maybe I am curious to know about you. Who are you? Where are you coming from? What's your story?" I asked. I was proud of my question, which kept my feeling of love in the background.

He thought for a few moments and asked, "What? Is it really important to know about me? I don't see any reason for this."

"There is every reason for this. You are my emancipator, and I do have every right to know about you," I retorted.

"Will you promise me that you will move away once you hear my story?" he inquired.

"Sure. I will do that. I am just eager to know about you—the stranger to my home with his bot and infinite knowledge," I said.

"You are just overestimating me. My story isn't that great. In fact, there are certain episodes I am not happy about," he replied.

"That doesn't matter. Just go on," I encouraged him.

I was really excited to know about him. In fact, I was very happy to be back in conversation with him. As he started to narrate his story, I was there totally, listening to him with a thousand ears.

Chapter 19: Tell Me Your Story

Aarav's Narration:

Not long ago, there were twins in a forest near Bandavgarh in Madhya Pradesh: a girl and a boy, inseparable siblings. They came into this world together to enjoy nature's bounty. And so, as soon as they grew a little, they didn't leave any part of the forest untouched with their play.

Always shouting each other's names—"Aarav...", "Amisha..."—till they echoed in the forest. Sometimes bathing in the brooks, sometimes jumping off the mini boulders, sometimes hanging on the trees, and sometimes swinging on saree-made swings, always high on their excitement, the little ones made sounds mightier than the roars of lions.

Why was this universe created? It was created so that we could play all the time and enjoy each other's company. Maa used to collect all the dry figs and dry wood, and cook us delicious meals. Babuji was not seen much; he was busy with his own work. Like nature, they were also providers for us.

We were four when the stars aligned. It meant that there was a boy somewhere in the jungle who had magical abilities and could perform miracles to save the world. And when a group of mystical creatures appeared, their bodies covered with ash powder and foreheads filled with turmeric and kastoori, I was hiding in our small hut, clutching my mother and sister tightly. Both of them could hear my fast heartbeat.

Little did I know that I was that boy with magical abilities until they stepped inside our house. The eldest one among the mystical creatures looked at me, with matted hair and eyes sunk deeply into his cheeks. He smiled as if he had discovered what he was seeking.

He then looked at my mother and said, “Mother, you have given birth to an amazing child who can do miracles and save the people from their hardships.”

My mother folded her hands as she understood what he was saying. She knew about this tradition of how families from tribes give away their children for the welfare of society during times of need. She also understood that it was now her turn. It was a blessing as God had chosen them, and it was a bane as we had to depart.

Though young, I understood the gravity of the situation. Those mystical creatures looked a little familiar to me. It was time to bid farewell to my mother and my sister. My mother hugged me for one last time, a frivolous one, knowing that we were cut off forever after this separation, without allowing tears to flow from her eyes. And then I gave a look to my sister, one which confused her, as she didn’t understand it.

Soon, they held my hand and directed me to their jeep, and off we started. And so began the running of my sister behind the jeep, her eyes crying rivers. She shouted my name—“Aaraaav... Aarav...”—so loud that it would have reached the heavens. I just kept looking at her as my vehicle browsed over the hilly terrain. The last image of my personal life etched in my heart is of that little girl crying for me before I entered into a new world.

Chapter 20: My New World

Some years had passed in the company of the mystics. I used to just observe them.

I was studying the dead when I was seven. How the life force leaves a body in various organisms, letting the organism dissolve into nature, astonished me. What astonished me even more was the arrogance—the ego of organisms when they are alive—thinking that this temporary life is forever. What astonished me beyond my wits was how sophisticated organisms like human beings don't ever try to understand their connection with nature and the cosmos, and just live a life ignorant of their full potential.

My training started with a week-long silence rite in a circle of burning pyres. The fire burned the bodies, mixed them with the five elements of nature, and released the spirit to the cosmos. The power of silence, away from the noisy herds of human beings, made me realize how arrogant the living ones are. Death can come to anyone at any time, and the dead will have to dissolve peacefully into nature. The whole purpose of a human being—the most intelligent living being that we know—is to gain knowledge of death and pass into that deep slumber peacefully, without arrogance, regret, or ego, or else our spirit may be released into the wrong portal. At the age of seven, I was astonished at this dissolution of life in death.

While I was astonished by death, I also learned to listen to the whispers of the spirits that left the bodies. I could already sense faint voices—gentle murmurs of those who had departed—telling me of their joys, regrets, and unfinished dreams. Some whispered like the rustling of leaves, others like the soft hum of flowing water. I learned to sit still, to let their words pass through me without fear.

By eight, my teachers took me deeper into the forest, where the pyres no longer burned but the silence was even more profound. There, I was taught to distinguish between the voices of nature and the voices of the departed. The wind carried lessons, the rivers sang of continuity, and the spirits spoke of release. I began to understand that death was not an end but a merging with the eternal rhythm of the cosmos.

At nine, my training grew more intense. I was asked to spend nights alone beneath the stars, listening not only to the spirits but to the vast silence of the universe itself. The constellations became my companions, and I felt the pulse of creation in the stillness. My mind grew sharper, my heart calmer. I realized that the whispers of the dead were not to frighten me but to remind me of the fragile arrogance of the living, who believed their temporary lives to be eternal.

By then, I was no longer just a child. I was becoming a listener of truths hidden in silence, a witness to the eternal bond between life, death, and the cosmos. But deep within me I felt the pain of separation from my twin sister.

One day, when I was silently listening to the fluttering of the fire, I heard a laugh—a little girl's laugh.
I asked, "Who are you?"
"Hey, so you can listen to me?" the little girl asked.
"Yes, I can. What's your name?" I asked. "I am Kali! Hehehe!" she chirped, her laughter echoing in that dark night.
"Kali, you have a cheerful laugh," I said.

"Hehehe!" she continued, "What's the point? I couldn't grow up big, at least like you, you old boy. I just passed away when I was six, in a stupid incident."

"You say that you are dead, but... you are still able to talk to me," I said.

"Everyone cannot listen to me. Only the chosen ones have this ability," she added.

"How can I help you, Kali?" I asked.

"You are the only one who has offered me help. Hehehe!" she laughed.

Our friendship grew with each passing day. I started listening to her and her painful story. It wrenched my heart to know that she was a six-year girl who had been sacrificed during a famine, offered to spirits to bring rain. She was deprived of her chance to live a human life, to learn and evolve, and she was now slowly evolving through understanding in her spirit form. Her soul had never crossed over after the sacrifice, and she was searching for the mukti mantra. Her story was like mine. We were both chosen ones—only I was alive and separated from my family, while she was dead and separated from her chance to live.

While the aghoras taught me mantras and chants, she taught me how to keenly listen to the dead, how to dreamwalk into our memories, and how to laugh in fear's face—because fear feeds the wrong spirits. She was my guru in the mystical world, though she didn't know how to free herself. I was her disciple, who also didn't know how to break free from the pain of separation from my twin sibling.

After some days, Kali became my shadow, invisible to others but always near me. Together, we tried to solve the complex puzzle of the physical world by studying it through keen observation.

Chapter 21: Dreamwalk And Descent Into Pretaloka

Some of the aghoras were astonished at my progress. They wondered how this boy of nine could sit in the darkest of nights in the graveyard, where dangerous spirits lurked. Some mystics were even jealous of me.

With the help of Kali, I gradually learned the dreamwalking technique and used it to heal my pain. It was a bridge between the arrogance of living with the truth of the dead. I walked into my dreams to meet Amisha. I watched her there, playing by the side of a tree, alone. I wanted to touch her and feel her, but I could never do it.

"Hehehe! You silly fellow. You are afraid to meet your loved one when she is still alive," Kali used to mock me.
"I cannot break the vows made to the mystics," I said.

When I was fourteen, one night, as I drifted into dreamwalking, the forest around me grew hazy, its shadows stretching long and restless. I searched for Amisha, and there she was—beneath a crooked tree, her small frame curled against its roots. But something was wrong. Her glow, once radiant like the morning sun, had dimmed. Her soul energy flickered like a dying lamp, each pulse weaker than the last.

The wrong spirits were feeding on her essence, and her major soul fragment had already been carried away. I didn't know what to do. This was not what I had ever expected for my twin soul—my other half fading into shadows while I stood helpless.

She became weak as she was separated from me. The balance of the cosmos was disturbed by the mystics.

"Oh! So the brother is sad. I see," mocked Kali, my shadow now.
"My sister is dying. I don't know what to do," I replied.
"You can be either sad, or you can do something about it. Hehehe!" she laughed hysterically—a laugh that made me think.
"What can I do, Kali? Please tell me," I requested.
"I will tell you if you promise to help me in return," she said.
"Okay, I will help you. What kind of help do you need?" I asked.
"You have to help me cross over after I help you in bringing the soul fragment. Is that a deal? Hehehe!" she asked.
"Cross over? Do you mean to get your spirit freed to the universe?"
"Yes, Aarav."
"Okay, Kali. I will help you do that. Tell me what I should do right now to save my sister."
"Aarav, when someone is turning weak suddenly, it means that their soul energy is being eaten by dark spirits. Your sister's major soul fragments have been taken away by those dark spirits to preta loka—the world of the departed, the world that exists between death and rebirth, the world beneath us."
"There is a portal to every loka, every world. Since you have promised to help me cross over to the higher world, I will help you go to the lower world," she said.

We went to a cremation ground at midnight, a time when wandering spirits lurk there. As instructed by Kali, I looked for a big Banyan tree. I drew a circle using ashes and bones as the door knob.

Just then, some aghoras came over and asked me, "What are you doing, child?"

"I am going to *preta loka* to save a life," I said.

"We forbid you from going there. It is only for the dead. When the living enters it, the *maya* will have you caught in it forever," they said.

"Isn't this world also full of *maya*? Aren't we able to live even then?" I asked.

"But the *maya* in the lower world is very tricky. Don't become one more spirit over there," they warned.

"I will take my chances when it comes to saving a life," I said.

"No one can stop a resolute one who is either doing good or bad. You will face the consequences of your karma." Saying this, they left.

We started our descent to *preta loka* with our meditation. It was an astral journey. Our physical bodies remained on the ground, while our mental ones undertook the actual journey to the lower world. The portal opened. Now, Kali was no longer a shadow—she took her form as a six-year-old. The fourteen-year-old and the six-year-old began their journey into the world of spirits. Who are spirits? Weren't they humans once, like Kali? Preta loka sounded more as a descent into the world of human arrogance and ignorance.

The World Of Unborns:

The eerie world of the unborn welcomed us. Darkness prevailed for a long time, pierced only by the relentless sound of crickets pounding in our ears. Then, suddenly, the cries of countless unborn souls struck us all at once. It was an ear-splitting, deafening wave of sorrow. Yet we knew we had to endure it to reach the final stage. There was no turning back.

Little Kali held my hand and said, "Aarav, pay attention to the noises and try to make meaning out of them. Don't fear it. This is the world of the unborn—the ones who were killed just before their birth. Listen carefully. Only by hearing them can we carry their truth forward. Only then will the path open further."

I looked at little Kali, amazed at her brilliance. Even as a spirit, she was evolving, bit by bit.

As I listened more closely, the noise began to take shape, and I could see their world faintly in a dim light. It was a place dominated by female unborns—perhaps because they were the ones most often killed before they could be born.

One voice cried, "Please, don't kill me!" Another pleaded, "What is my mistake? I will bring you happiness, like a flower blooming in your garden. Please don't get rid of me." And on and on went the desperate pleadings of the unborn. Our eyes wept rivers, but we could not stop there. We had to move forward.

"They're not just voices, Aarav," Kali said softly. "They're questions we never dared to answer."

I remained silent in that sorrowful world. Yet in their cries, I heard not only pain but also the echo of choices made in silence—choices that never asked what joy might have bloomed. I could feel humanity's ego-driven decision to kill unborn girls, a choice that shattered the cosmic balance of the universe again and again. These unborn souls embodied the arrogance of denying life its chance to evolve.

What true difference lies in having a male child or a female child? Life itself is a miracle, not its form. Yet how blind and arrogant human behaviour becomes when it turns away from right knowledge. In clinging to illusions of superiority, humanity forgets that every soul—whether born as boy or girl—is a fragment of the same cosmic light, destined to evolve and complete the balance of existence.

<u>The World Of Dead Children:</u>

Next came the world of dead children. It was, in truth, Kali's world, but she had escaped from it through her relentless efforts. Many others, however—as far as my eyes could see—remained trapped there. The air carried the scent of forgotten toys and lullabies. Shadows giggled behind broken swings. Their laughter was light—too light—like echoes of dreams never dreamt.

They wanted to play with us. Just play and play, with all the chirpy laughs of "hehehe!", just like Kali. We played with them for a while, but they would not let us move forward. They wanted us to stay with them, as children do. Kali grew furious, for our time was running short. I sat down and pleaded with them earnestly, as I would with any adult. I explained my position as a twin brother and spoke of the anguish my sister was enduring.

Kali said, "You are wasting time. Children can't understand adults."

But within moments, they gave us the way. Some even had tears in their eyes. One child stepped forward, eyes wide with something older than time. "We know what it means to be left behind. Go and save her, so she doesn't become one of us."

We walked away, bidding them farewell. Kali whispered, "I thought children couldn't understand grown-ups."

"Children can understand grown-ups like us if we start treating them as equals. It is only a myth that they cannot," I said.

Kali looked back at the children, her voice softer than usual. "Maybe I never truly escaped them. Maybe I only began to explore more, and that is why I was able to step out from here.

How I wish every grown-up treated all children as equals! I would never have been offered as a sacrifice if they had asked my decision. That sacrifice robbed me of my dignity and my chance to live."

The World Of Regrets:

Next, we entered the world of regrets. These were adults who had died burdened with remorse. Most were unaware of our presence, lost in endless weeping over their regrets.
One soul cried, "Had I forgiven him, I would have been free!"
Another, who noticed us, shouted, "Oh, lucky you! You will never be a part of us, for you have taken a path of no regrets for your loved one. We are stuck here eternally."
One spirit, envious of our journey, did something strange. Kali sensed it and warned me, "Aarav, it's... it's latching onto you!"
I looked at her, confused. I felt something entering me. I had a strong personality, but in the world of pretas, anything was possible. I existed in my body, yet at the same time another spirit latched onto me.
Kali laughed at my new demeanor. "Aarav, you look funny when you walk seriously."
"Who are you? Why are you calling me Aarav? I am not Aarav. I am Nishabdh. I need a body to return to the physical world and live my unfulfilled life," Nishabdh said.
I was still inside my body, witnessing everything. Kali looked at me strangely.
"If you are Nishabdh, where is Aarav?" she asked.
"He has gone. I have sent him away," he answered.
"What? How can you do that?" Kali shouted furiously.
Then my body collapsed as if dead. It was time for a dialogue between me and Nishabdh. Kali didn't understand any of this and simply sat near me, cradling my head in her lap.

"Hey Nishabdh, you can't take over my body."
"I can. I can do anything."
"If you have taken over my body, why am I still here?"
He was silent.
"I will leave my body only when I am dead. You do not have the power to kill me," I said.
"But I can make you weak and silent, and dominate you as I am doing now. Not even your voice comes out of your body when I am here. Did you see that?" Nishabdh replied.
"Dear, that is because I am allowing you to dominate me. I understand your pain of regret. But since this is preta loka, you have the power to enter and stay inside me. Yet as soon as I return to the world of humans, you can do nothing. It is an eternal truth that no one can truly influence another person. Those who are influenced give up their power of reason to those who try to control them. Real knowledge is earned only by breaking the barrier of self. That is the only way to free a person. So, you staying inside me won't work."
"I regret not having the simple knowledge of using my mind. All my life I did what society told me, and I regret it deeply. I want to fix it. What should I do?"
"Work on yourself. Form goals. Don't just live in the past—work toward your goals," I said.
"What could be the goals for a regretful spirit?" Nishabdh asked.
"You feel regret because you chose it. Feeling regretful has been your goal for a long time. Now it's time to deny the past and begin anew. It's hard, but not impossible. Start a life without regrets, with small actionable goals that bring happiness. That is the best thing to do right now," I answered.
Nishabdh said nothing further. He simply left my body. And I returned, waking up in Kali's lap, where her tears streamed

down her face. When she saw me, a smile carved itself onto her lips.

"I thought I lost you!" she said.

"No, I am here to get the soul fragment, and I won't go anywhere," I said, rising.

We walked past the world of regrets. Kali looked back one last time and said, "What a messy world this is. When alive, they couldn't do what was right—now they regret."

<u>The World Of Memories:</u>

Next, we moved into the world of memories—a beautiful realm of mirrors. As far as our eyes could see, there were countless mirrors, each reflecting a memory from our lives. Kali saw herself as a child playing in the forests, while I saw myself playing alongside my sister. In some mirrors, we glimpsed our parents and the houses we had grown up in. The sight filled us with nostalgia. Then we came upon the largest mirror of all. It held the most important memory of anyone who stood before it.

Kali faced her most important memory. She saw herself being handed over to the sophists, who claimed they could bring rain if a girl child was offered to the spirits. Her parents reluctantly agreed. Her mother broke down in tears, while Kali closed her eyes, trembling in fear during the final act.

Next, I stood before the mirror. It revealed my mother singing a lullaby to my sister and me—sweeter than the murmur of brooks, sweeter even than the songs of the *koyals*. "Look, Kali, how beautiful my family is!" I exclaimed. Kali smiled.

"I feel like I should just sit here forever," I added.

Kali remained silent for a few moments, lost in her own memories. Then realization struck her—a new learning for both of us.

She said, "Aarav, these are memories, not realities. Though memories are beautiful, one should not live in them forever. All the dead, all the past, is over—like a sweet dream dreamt in sleep. So do not wish to live in memories."

I understood what she meant.

"Then, what should I do now?" I asked.

"It is the mirror of sacrificial memory," she said, gazing at the magnificent mirror that displayed the most important memory of our lives.

I looked at her, confused.

"It demands the sacrifice of your most beautiful memory. This is the final stage of our journey. Only this sacrifice will allow you to reclaim the soul fragment."

I thought for a few moments, then knelt before the mirror, joined my hands, and closed my eyes.

The world of mirrors dissolved, and in place of the great mirror appeared a tiny flame, glowing like a firefly.

"That is the soul fragment of your twin sister," said Kali.

Her voice had changed, sounding more mature. She realized she had been living in the memories of her haunted past, and that it was time to move beyond them.

I took the soul fragment and placed it safely in my pocket. Together, we closed our eyes—and soon, we were back in the physical world.

***

As we opened our eyes, a new morning slowly lit up the horizon. I removed the soul fragment from my pocket and released it into the sky. It rose into the air like a firefly of the

day. I knew it would return to my sister, and she would be safe. I will dreamwalk and check on her this evening, I thought.
As I walked away, Kali—my shadow—asked, "So, which memory did you sacrifice?"
"The lullaby of my mother, sweeter than the murmur of brooks and even sweeter than the songs of the koyal," I replied.
"Ah ha! I am a dead spirit, yet I still remember my mother's lullaby. See, I am happier than you!" Kali teased, trying to lighten my mood.
I smiled.
"So, did it rain after you were sacrificed?" I asked her.
"No. It didn't. Why didn't it rain, Aarav?" she asked, sounding a little confused.
"Because everything happens through karma. If one desires rain, they must perform good karma—like planting trees and caring for nature. Instead, they believed magic would solve the problem."
Kali smiled. We both sounded more mature after our journey through Preta Loka.

Just then, Kali cried out in pain. "Something is happening to me. I feel like something is pulling me in!"
"What? What's happening, Kali?" I asked.
"I don't know, Aarav. Something is dragging me... Argh!"
Crying in agony, Kali trembled—and then, in an instant, she vanished.

Chapter 22: Illusion Of Fake Power, Kali Crosses Over

I was puzzled, unable to understand what had happened to Kali. Had she gone back to *Preta Loka*? I called out to her for some time, searching every corner of the cremation grounds and meadows. No reply came. Instead, I noticed a mystic, a man in his forties, standing far away, smiling. Something in me felt he had a hand in this.

I ran toward him as he began to walk away. Catching up, I asked, "Hey, guruji! Can I talk with you?"

"Speak, lad," he said.

"Sir, until now I was interacting with one spirit—her name was Kali. Suddenly she vanished. She said she felt like something was sucking her in. Can you tell me what might have happened to her?"

"Child, first of all, spirits do not have names," he replied.

"But she did," I insisted.

He continued, ignoring me.

"Spirits are not meant to be befriended. They are to be subjugated and used for greater purposes," he said with authority.

"Why do you think so, sir? What do you plan to use this spirit for?"

"Haha! I will become the most powerful. By harnessing the pretas from Preta Loka, I can unleash great powers. This spirit will be my compass to reach there," he said.

I clenched my fists. His words felt like poison—not just to Kali, but to everything she stood for. The arrogance of human beings clinging on to the ideas of fake wealth baffled me beyond my wits! The mystic chuckled, his eyes gleaming with hunger. My heart pounded. Was Kali taken because of me?

He raised a small amulet—blackened, pulsing faintly. A chill crawled down my spine.
"Inside this," he said, "she is my key to Preta Loka's deepest vaults—the ones even you haven't seen. I can build a preta army and rule over the dead."
I stared at the amulet. I could feel her presence—faint, flickering, like a candle in a storm.
"You don't understand what you're doing," I said. "Preta Loka isn't a treasure chest. It's a wound. You don't conquer it—you heal it."
The mystic laughed again, but hollowly. Something in my voice unsettled him.
"You speak like a sage, but you're just a boy," he sneered.
"Then let me show you what a boy can do," I whispered.
I quickly gathered ash dust from the ground, held it in my open palm, blew it into the air, and chanted the Achetan Mantra.
"Wait! What are you doing?" the mystic shouted.
The dust swirled, glowing briefly, and struck him in the chest. He stumbled, eyes wide, and collapsed unconscious.
I didn't wait. I seized the amulet, gripped it tightly, and whispered, "Forgive me, Kali." With all my strength, I smashed it against a stone slab.

The amulet cracked—then shattered, revealing horsehair and the nails of dead dogs that had caged her. One final blow would release her, but I would need to chant the Mukti Mantra—the emancipation chant that would help her cross over. I had hidden this truth from her all along. I hadn't lied, but I had spoken as if mukti never existed. Now she would know, and her departure would be more painful. But I had to do it.
I struck the final blow.

The spirit emerged—a smiling little girl of six. Just before crossing into the other world, she appeared like a shimmering image and spoke words that will stay with me forever:
"I know you knew the Mukti Mantra all along. I was as afraid of leaving you as you were of losing me."
"I think everyone knows Mukti Marg. It is simple: forgive all sins—those of others and your own. Do not carry hatred, regret, or memory with you," I said.
"Some memories are special. You lost one for your sister. And now, I will lose yours," Kali replied.
"I will miss you, Kali."
And there it was—her freedom, her emancipation. And with her dissolution, from that day onwards, the world became a little more beautiful.

The mystic awoke, glaring at me.
"You know you just lost the chance to become the most powerful person in the world?"
"You have a wrong notion of power, sir," I said.
"What is power then? Tell me, you knowledgeable fool!" he shouted, holding and shaking my shoulders.
"True power is the freedom to do anything in the universe, but choosing only responsible actions. You already have all the power in this universe, sir," I said calmly.
He looked at me, said nothing, and walked away.

As I left, the sun shone brightly. My shadow was just my shadow—it was no longer Kali. I realized I had come into this world alone, and I would leave it alone. I would not even carry memories with me. Perhaps that is why no one remembers their past lives.

As I walked, I realized I could no longer dreamwalk without Kali's support. Loneliness settled in. Though the mystics had brought me here and my training was complete, they told me my goal now was to find a purpose. But I was terrible at forming new goals.

It was sheer luck that I met Kali, who became my companion all these years. Now, I was unwilling to meet anyone else, for every meeting would only lead to another farewell.

Sometimes, gazing at the burning pyres, sometimes at the cawing crows, sometimes at the living human beings, I wondered: *What is life? Why were we created?*

Each time I asked this question, life asked it back to me. Even if the body dies and the spirit lives, there is still life. But what is its purpose? Seeking that answer became the purpose of my existence.

I thought of it constantly—while walking through forests, meditating by riverbanks, or gazing at the serene beauty of the earth from mountaintops. The question always returned.

And one day, I decided to listen for the answer in everything I encountered. I stood near a great tree, its branches drooping so low that some brushed my shoulders. I bent down, pressed my ear against a new leaf, and it told me a story—its real story. This is the story of that leaf, told by itself.

Chapter 23: A New Leaf's Story

****New leaf starts narrating its story ****

***

It was my first day. I was very small, tiny, and light green in colour. The world looked fascinating to my eyes. The winds tickled me playfully, and the sunlight filled me with warmth and joy. I saw other leaves, a little older than me, dark green in colour. They were just as happy as I was. We were all nourished by the mother root. She sent her nourishment through the thick brown trunk, which passed it to the branches. The branches sent it to the twigs, and the twigs finally sent it to us. Each day felt merrier than the one before. But after some days, I noticed that certain leaves began to turn yellow—fading more and more with each passing day. Then, one day, a sweet, melancholic music filled the air around us. It was the most beautiful music, yet it made us nostalgic, trembling with a reminder of something ancient. I could never understand what that ancient thing was, but it felt like a sweet pain. I watched as the yellowest leaves broke away from the twigs and drifted slowly to the ground, dancing to that music. And then, the music stopped.

I was not sure what this meant. I looked at the other leaves, but they only said, "Don't worry, little one. It is common." Their answer did not satisfy me, for my heart raced with questions. So I asked the twig I was hanging from, "What was that music? I am so scared of it." The twig passed my question to the branch, the branch to the trunk, and the trunk to the mother root.

Sensing my fear, the mother root sent back a message through the trunk, then to the branches, and finally to the twig. The twig whispered to me:

"Mother root says this: *Little one, you are here to play and enjoy your time. This earth is a heaven created for us. The winds are here to caress us, the sunlight to refresh us, and the water to nourish us. Do not doubt this. Your purpose is to play and to learn to choose happiness every moment. Is happiness really that important? Yes—it is the most beneficial feeling, keeping you in good health more than any other emotion. Playfulness and happiness are essential.*

I know you fear the sweet, melancholic music that makes us tremble and stand tall. But do not be afraid. It is only a reminder that our time is ticking, urging us to play more and be happier than ever. There is no time to dwell on the past—the past is dead and should not haunt you. The future is only an illusion until it arrives, so do not dread it either. Believe me: play and be happy. When the time comes, you will fall to the ground listening to that sweet music. Then I will take you into my eternal embrace and give you a new shape, a new form of life. Even if your time to fall never comes because of some magical advancement, it is still your responsibility to cling to the mother tree, to play, and to be happy—for that is the best choice one can make in life."

Since then, I have only played and chosen happiness in my own way. Sometimes I punch the older leaves in their sides, sometimes I dance in the breeze. I make faces at the sun and wave at the passing clouds. The chirping of birds makes me laugh, and the rain makes me laugh even more with its strange sounds. The sweetest music of all, for me, is the one that plays when the leaves fall, dancing to the ground. And the most beautiful moment is every moment in which I make a choice—the choice to stay happy.

Let the whole world come to an end; I will hug my mother and remain happy.

New leaf ends its story and Aarav's narration resumes

***

Something changed in me from that moment onward. I stopped chasing things—chasing knowledge, chasing memories, chasing anything at all. Instead, I smiled and lived in the present. I chose wisely, embracing only what brought me happiness. I let go of the past because I was done with it. My sister was safe. Kali was gone. My most cherished memory of my mother's lullaby was lost. Yet I refused to make excuses for sadness or use those incidents as reasons to grieve. I released them. They were sweet phases—sweet, painful phases of my life. Now, I chose happiness deliberately.

I learned only what gave me joy. I built a talking bot by studying technology, and it became my artificial companion. I read books that fascinated me. Every night I gazed at the stars, and every day I set new goals that helped me stay happy. And I grew.

When I was twenty-eight, a mystic found me—a rare encounter in my life. He told me he was working on supernatural projects and believed my skills could serve humanity. Little did I know he would send me here, to your haunted house on the hill. And from here, you already know my story.

Aarav completed narrating his story. Chennamma resumes the discussion.

PART FOUR

Chapter 24: I Want Form

The story of the stranger filled me with awe. With him sitting over there, brushing his hair now and then, smiling at times, thinking by scratching his forehead during some thoughtful moments was a beautiful thing for me to witness. His tone had some connection with my soul. My soul felt alive when he spoke.

Our exchange of stories was heartfelt. I sensed that we truly understood each other, that we could have made a fine pair. But I was a soul, and he was a living human. I didn't know how to bridge that gap.

Just then, his voice pulled me out of my reverie.

"Chennamma, are you there?"

"Yes, Aarav, I am here."

"So, that's my story. You are the first person to hear it," he said.

"I'm glad to be that. I'm happy you've found your strength in choosing happiness."

He smiled—a genuine smile, born of true feeling.

"So, what's next?" he asked.

"I don't know," I admitted.

"You should cross over, Chennamma," he said.

I knew it was what I needed, but I felt unfinished. I was too afraid to admit my love for him.

"Are you there, Chennamma?" he asked again.

"Yes." My reply sounded hesitant.

"What's your doubt? Don't hold it back. Ask me, and then cross over," he urged.

"You mustn't laugh if I tell you what I'm feeling," I said.

"Hmm. Okay," he replied, suspiciously.

"I think I'm in love with you."

"What?" His face turned frantic.

"I thought you would laugh at my proposal."
"What are you saying? How can you possibly love me? I'm a human being, and you are a gh..." He stopped, then continued, "You are a soul spirit."
"Go ahead and say it—I'm a ghost. It doesn't matter."
"No, I didn't want to hurt you. It just slipped out."
"It's fine. I don't mind. I've moved beyond my ghostly nature because of you. Your gentle presence dispelled my darkness. No one, except my mother, has ever spoken to me the way you have," I said.
"But Chennamma, just because I spoke sincerely doesn't mean you should fall in love with me. If that were true, every woman I spoke to would fall in love with me, wouldn't they?" he said, still confused.
A ghost proposing to a human was rare—almost impossible.
"You're overthinking. Why assume you'll speak to so many women, and that all of them would fall in love with you?" I chuckled.
He paused, muttering to himself, "Why would I speak to so many women, and why would they all love me?" Then he admitted, "Look, Chennamma, I don't know. I just said that to win the argument and discourage you from loving me."
"That's correct," I said calmly.
"See, you're a soul spirit, and I'm a human who has vowed celibacy," he argued.
"So what? I love you. I only want to spend a few moments with you. I'm not seeking physical pleasures," I replied.
Then he said something silly: "Do you know you were born in the '70s, and I was born in '97? We have an age gap of 27 years."
I laughed. But then he added something that struck me. "And you were married."
My laughter stopped. I grew serious.

"Answer me, stranger. Did I marry in my right mind?"
"No."
"Did I know my husband's nature before marriage?"
"No."
"Did he treat me well?"
"No."
"Did he and his family exploit us, believing our lands hid the Nizam's treasure?"
"Yes."
"Didn't they separate me from my mother? Wasn't that a crime?"
"Yes, it was."
"And finally, didn't they burn me alive? Wasn't that the most heinous act?"
"Yes, it was. But they were ignorant—terribly ignorant. You must forgive them to cross over," he said.
"I know. But tell me—did you ever see me experience love for anyone, apart from my mother?"
"No."
"True love finds a heart rarely. And it found mine when we began speaking. It's boundless, and I cannot stop feeling it."
"I understand you, Chennamma, but..."
I interrupted, smiling at the sound of my name. "Don't say 'but.' Say 'yes.'"
"Chennamma, you cannot force me."
"This is the last thing I'll ask."
"To love you back?"
"That's the second last. The first is this: give me a human form. I want to walk beside you, sit with you—maybe on a mountain top, maybe by a riverbank."
"That's all?" he asked curiously.
"And... maybe a kiss?" I added.

"What are you saying?" He covered his face with his hands, annoyed.
"Treat this as society's repentance. It never gave me a chance to live my own life. A physical form, even for a few moments, would let me be with you. I've been madly in love, but without a beating heart. That feels strange. I don't want to cross over with regrets. That's why I'm asking," I said, fiercer than before.
"But our ages?"
"Age is just a number when it comes to the love of souls."
"If you love my soul, why want a physical form?"
"So I can feel a heart beating in love. Is that wrong?"
"No. It's not wrong. It's just against society's norms."
"So, are you driven by society?"
"No. I'm driven by my heart."
"Then what does your heart say about my proposal?" I asked.
He thought deeply.
"What you ask isn't wrong, but it's beyond my understanding," he said.
"Aarav, you've spoken meaningfully with a ghost like me. You've journeyed to Preta Loka with a six-year-old spirit and brought back your sister's soul fragment. You've listened to birds and trees for wisdom. You always attempt the impossible. Now, try for me," I said.
"I do love attempting the impossible. But the question is—'is it right?'"
"It is. Love is the most righteous pursuit. Those who cannot express love live with regrets of 'could have beens' and 'would have beens.' I didn't want that, so I expressed mine."
"And what about heartbreak? What if love isn't returned?" he asked.
"If you don't love me, it's okay. I won't force you. I won't even be carrying your memory once I cross over. It's just the longing

that makes me want a form – the longing to experience your company like an ordinary human being," I said earnestly.
Silence filled the air. He was lost in thought.
"So?" I asked.
"You've put me in a difficult situation."
"It's simple. Say yes or no. Express what you feel," I said.
"Okay. I'll give you a form, but it may last only for a few moments. Is that fine?"
"Hmm... does that mean you love me too?" I teased, my heart bubbling with joy.
"I love this universe profoundly. And you are a part of it—an important part that has been denied love at every step. If I can fill that void, if I can be a reason for your happiness, then I would feel like the sun—whose presence helps so many flourish. Just as the sun loves to light up the world with its warmth, I love you," he said.
Had I had lips, they would have stretched into a smile as wide as a rainbow.
"I love you too," I said, after a pause.
He smiled.
"So, what are we waiting for?" I asked, feeling like the driver of this love story.
Aarav scratched his beard and pushed his hair back.
"Tom, wake up."
His bot restarted.
"Was he in sleep mode all this time? Did he miss everything we said?" I asked.
"No, miss. I heard it all. I thought my boss would never fall in love. But you did the impossible."
"Hey Tom, we have work. Turn the pages to how God created a woman."

Tom wasn't just a talking bot, as I had assumed. He burst into a glow, scattering light in every direction, and projected a floating collection of books above him. He looked less like a machine and more like a walking library. Aarav navigated through the books—sometimes swiping with his fingertips, other times issuing crisp voice commands—searching for the one he needed.

Chapter 25: Break The Rules

The discussion between Aarav and Tom was at its peak on how a human being was created, and that too how especially a woman was created by the supreme God.

"Tom, show me the ancient books. The ones that speak of how the Supreme crafted woman—not just born, but *woven*."

Tom said while he was working on the commands, *"Accessing cosmic archives... Displaying holographic manuscripts from the Vault of Origins."*

Books floated around them like little stars, each glowing with its unique light. After flipping through some books, they halted at one.

"This one is humming the song of creation," said Tom.

The book which Tom suggested was radiating the images of galaxies, oceans, and some magical embryonic light. It was a sight to see their work.

I couldn't believe what I was seeing. From the book, Aarav was even able to pick out a spoon and a bowl – a bowl of silence, and a spoon of intent. With the spoon in one hand and bowl in another, he flipped through the pages through his voice commands.

"Boss, that's an interesting choice. You are planning to mix the elements manually. That's old school alchemy," said Tom.

Aarav was lost in the process of creation and didn't respond. As he flipped through the various pages of that resplendent book, he gave short voice commands, each word made the process look even more magical.

"Sunlight" he commanded.

A spoonful of golden warmth floated into the bowl of silence.

"Soil."

A pinch of soil with ancient memory settled beside it.

"Wind."

The breathing power danced in.

"Ocean."

A drop of emotion rippled into the mixture.

"Aarav, you are blending the five elements. But, what about the soul's palette?"

"Partial soul is already available here. For the missing soul fragment, let me do this," he said.

He smiled and pulled out the painter's brush from the book's spine.

"Let's add feeling," he said.

He dipped the brush into a rainbow from the book and chose the colours of joy, sorrow, courage, and grace and put them into the bowl. Then he stirred them.

"Colour calibration complete. Emotional balance, complete," said Tom.

Then Aarav called out for a white cloth. It was soft as moonlight and woven with the threads of possibility.

What I was seeing was beyond imagination.

He wrapped the bowl's contents into this cloth gently, like wrapping a new born baby into it.

"Chennamma, this cloth will be your dress once you gain form. It is not stitched for shape, it is tailored for the soul. That's why it is called the cloth of possibility."

I stood there speechless. The process wasn't just mystical, it was very intimate.

"Creation sequence complete. Awaiting emergence," Tom said.

"She's not just emerging. She's arriving—with memory, meaning, and mystery," said Aarav, smiling at his creation.

Just then, Tom stopped.
"Boss, there is an incoming message for you."
"Who is it, Tom?" Aarav asked.
"It is your boss, Rudranetra."
"Take the call," he commanded. His boss was online.

"Aarav, what are you doing?" Rudra asked in an angry authoritative tone.
"I am just doing my duty. This ghost catching project will be finished in sometime," Aarav answered.

"But, what are you actually doing? Why are you giving a physical body to a soul? That is not why I sent you there."
"Sir, I totally understand why you have sent me here. But as the event unfolded, I am at this leg of the journey. I know what I am doing. You have to trust me sir," Aarav said.
"Aarav, I don't have any doubt on you. But, the soul to which you are going to give a physical form will get unlimited powers. And the true nature of a being is revealed when it is awarded all the powers in the universe. You may be creating a powerful monster!"
"Sir, if we don't give the opportunity to someone by trusting that someone, then how will that someone ever realise their true potential. When we elect a leader, we are giving total powers of our affairs to that leader. If we don't give, how will the leader perform the affairs to his best. If we love someone, we have to trust and place our life in their hands, like a child does with its parents. Only then, we can experience true love from that someone. Guruji, we have to submit ourselves completely, to see the true power of our creation."
"Aarav, what you are saying is true. But keeping the impending dangers, one must stop those creations which may bring destruction. So, I order you to stop this operation immediately."
"Sir, I have taken a pledge to do this. And I have complete belief in what I am creating. It will not be misutilized. I cannot stop right now."
"Then, I am coming to stop you!" he cut the call in anger.

For a moment, I was taken aback. Because of my weird selfish request, Aarav had to go through the anger of his employer.
"Hey, Aarav, is it going to be a problem?" I asked.

"Chennamma, it doesn't matter. We are free souls. And we have planned things that are right and that are good. So, no one should have any objection. My employer is worrying because this act of creation will give you not only a momentary physical body but also limitless powers. He is convinced that you will use those powers to harm the world."
"He is right in worrying according to him. What if I go rogue after attaining limitless powers? Shall we cancel the plan?" I asked doubtfully.
"All feelings of powerfulness are illusions. Freedom tied with the threads of responsibilities is the only true nature of any power. I have complete faith in you that you will cross over after this final thing I am doing for you."
I thought for some time. Then said, "okay."

"Tom, how long would it take for Rudra to reach here?" Aarav asked.
"Maybe, half an hour."
"The process of creation?"
"Emergence is pending. It will take 45 minutes."
"Let's get started."

Aarav started to chant words that I couldn't understand. But those words had a peculiar power that filled me with warmth. I was feeling as if I was in the lap of my mother. Then, I felt as if I were in my mother's cozy womb again. I was looking at the stranger who just came yesterday and became the love of my life.
He was just lost in his work. In many ways, he was like my mother who went through many difficult situations for my wellbeing. And now, he was fighting with the world for me. He wasn't fighting for his ego, he was fighting for what is right and

what is good for me. While he was lost in his work, I kept gazing at him like the sunflower that gazes at the sun in awe. And during this process, I started humming something beautiful in myself.

When the cool wind breezes by,
I long to sit beside you.
When stars twinkle across the sky,
I yearn to rest my head on your shoulder.
I wish to move so close to you -
So close that you and I are just one breath, one heartbeat.
And I find my ending on your lips,
Like a sweet song,
Or the curve of your beautiful smile.

Almost thirty minutes passed. I could feel someone stand near the house.

"Rudranetra has arrived," said Tom.

Rudranetra had an authoritative demeanour. He also had long hair but the gentleness that Aarav had was missing in him. I could clearly sense that he was angry.

"Turn or the shield of love," commanded Aarav.

"Shield of love activated," said Tom.

Just then a mystic light surrounded the house like a semi spherical water bubble.

Seeing this, Rudranetra became furious. He tried to enter into the premises of the house but the shield obstructed him. Fury was reaching the stage of rage now. He lifted both his hands up and was able to generate a laser beam kind of fire. He directed it on to the shield.

Aarav continued his work. I continued my hum.

When the colorful flowers bloom,
And the birds sing their melodious songs,
Let me draw closer to you—inch by inch,
Let me cleanse the sorrows nestled in your heart,
And then let me descend like the rain—
a rain of nectar, bathing you in love and light.

"Boss!" Tom interrupted.
Aarav looked at Tom.
"The shield is under attack from Rudranetra."
"How long can our shield withstand this attack?" asked Aarav.
"Maybe, 20 minutes," said Tom.
"Our work will be over in 10 minutes. It should be fine," he continued his work. I continued my hum.

Lives are flowing rivers,
You and I—just two strangers drifting near.
But when we meet and journey together,
It becomes a beautiful journey through time.
Sharing our sorrows and joys alike
Makes our bond stronger, gentler, and pure.
Even the storms feel softer when you're beside me,
And nights glow radiantly with warmth of love.
And I find my ending on your lips,
Like a sweet song,
Or the curve of your beautiful smile.

Just then, I was sucked in the whirlwind of some mysterious force. As I was rapidly moving in that whirlwind, all my memories came flooding back. The memories of my brave mother, my village, my school, and my growing up – all the happy memories resurfaced. The memories of my father trying to bubble me, landlords coming to my house to intimidate me, and the greedy faces of my husband and my mother in law who eventually burned me – all the sad ones resurfaced too. But all of these are past now. I was taking a new form.

The last thing I remember hearing from Aarav and Tom is "Emergence complete" from Tom.

Chapter 26: The Eclogue

I could not see anything like before. For a moment, I missed the power of seeing everything like a ghost. I had a thousand eyes back then. But wait, what was it? I was lying on the floor on my stomach. The cloth – the cloth of possibilities draped over me like a blanket. I could feel my hands and my fingers. I touched my face with them. Then, I could feel the body I was waiting for. But hesitation overwhelmed my heart. How can I get up? I was not even properly dressed. The stranger may be standing right next to see me – to see the miracle he created.

Then, I sensed something amazing. Without even getting up, I could see him. I could see Tom. I could also see his arrogant employer who was still trying to break the shield outside the house. Maybe, these were the limitless powers they were talking about. The word 'Power' fascinated me for a moment but the pull of 'love' was stronger.

I got up from the ground and the cloth of possibility fit me as a beautiful dress of rainbow. And there I stood in human form in front of the one whom I loved. We stood amidst the struggle between the shield of love and the dagger of rage.

"Love shield is yielding. Alert!" shouted Tom.

Aarav looked at me in awe. I was feeling shy. Whether his shield of love will yield to his employer's dagger or not, my heart had already yielded to his gaze.

"Chennamma, you look beautiful.." he said.

"Love shield is yielding. Alert!" shouted Tom, one more time.

As time was running out, I held Aarav's hand, and in a flash of light we soared above the rooftop of the house. His physical body remained behind, but I created another form for him, and together we drifted among the clouds. The feeling of limitless power was exhilarating. As the winds rushed across our faces, he brushed his hair back over his ears, still looking confused.

"Where are you taking me?" he asked, eyes gleaming with wonder and suspicion.
"Somewhere you'll like," I said.
"But where?" he pressed again.

In a few moments, we landed in a forest. I watched him as he gazed across the familiar trees.
"This is the place where I grew up!" he said, a smile spreading across his face.
"Yes. Let's go inside. Let's meet your family," I replied.
He smiled at me, but hesitated.
"I've vowed never to have a family," he said.
"Hmm. That's a problem," I paused. "But this isn't you. This is a new human form I created for you—just as you created me. Those vows don't apply now."
He looked confused.
"Let's move forward," I urged, nudging him to step ahead.

Soon, we walked into the area where his family once lived. The expressions crossing his face told me my surprise was worth it. He touched the low branches, splashed water from the brooks, stood on small boulders to catch the sunlight darting through the forest. And then, he saw his house.

Just then, a sweet melody filled the air.
"This is the lullaby my mother used to sing for us," he whispered. The memory pierced his heart, tears of joy welling in his eyes.
"You know this is the memory I sacrificed to get the soul fragment back," he said.
"I know," I replied, holding his hands. "Now, you'll never forget it," I said looking into his eyes while walking towards his house. "Go in. Meet your loved ones," I said.

He held my hand and led me to the entrance. A woman's voice carried the lullaby from inside.
"Hello, is someone there?" Aarav called.
"Hush! Someone has come," the woman whispered to the child, then stepped out with a baby in her arms.
The baby giggled at us. "Yes?" she asked.
We stood frozen. Aarav was speechless at the sight of his twin sister.
"Yes? What do you want?" she asked again.
"We're lost in the forest. Can you show us the way out?" I said, because Aarav couldn't speak.
Her eyes lingered on Aarav's face. The baby reached out toward him with tiny fingers. Amisha tilted her head, recognition flickering.
"You look… familiar. Very familiar. If I had my brother with me today, I think he would look just like you," she said.
"I've just lost my way," he murmured.
"We have lost our way," I corrected gently.
"Can we have some water?" Aarav asked.
"Of course. Please sit," she said, disappearing inside.

We sat in the verandah. It was a house like mine, with open space and a mirror hanging on one side. I stood before it, checking myself.

"Aarav, do I look fine?" I asked.

"You look beautiful," he said.

"Beautiful enough to break your vow of celibacy?" I teased.

He smiled, silent.

Amisha returned with a jug of water and a glass. She set the baby down, who stared at me. I made faces, and she giggled.

"So, what's your name? Where are you from?" she asked.

"I'm Abhiram," he lied softly, "from a nearby city."

I shot him a wide-eyed look, but he ignored it.

"My brother's name was... is Aarav," she said, correcting herself. "If he had grown up, he would look just like you." Tears threatened her voice.

"Where did he go?" Aarav asked.

"The mystics took him when we were children. We played endlessly, inseparable since birth. But on the day the stars aligned, they came and took him away. He stared at me from the jeep as I screamed, 'Brother, don't go!' running behind it. But he disappeared that day," she said.

"Hmm... maybe his purpose was something else," Aarav said.

"Maybe," she whispered.

"But he used to come in my dreams often. We would talk and play there. It lasted for many days," she said.

"Oh, that sounds interesting," he replied.

"And then I fell very sick. Even the doctors gave up hope. Amma was drowning in tears."

"What happened then?"

"Something mysterious. No one knew what it was. I just recovered. The doctors called it a miracle," she said.

"I'm glad you became well," Aarav said, knowing the truth of the soul fragment.
"But from that day, something broke between me and the universe. My brother never came into my dreams again. I felt forgotten."
He stayed silent. He knew it was the sacrifice of the lullaby and Kali's cross over that severed their bond.
"Where is your mother?" he asked.
"She passed away a few years ago, after my marriage."
"I'm sorry," he said. I thought he must have known about his mother's death so he didn't pay much attention to it.

Though I played with the baby, I heard everything.
"Please don't mind, stranger. Seeing you made me feel reconnected to the universe. That's why I shared my story," Amisha said, tears softening her eyes.
"You can always treat me as your brother," Aarav said.
"It's time to go," I interrupted. My physical form was fading; I had only moments left.
Aarav bid farewell to his sister and nephew with a genuine smile—the very reason I had brought him here. Amisha explained the route to the highway, though we didn't need it.

We walked back into the forest, alone again. I felt like we were the only two souls in the universe.
"Why did you do this, Chennamma? Why make me meet my sister?" he asked, still overwhelmed by the reunion and the return of his mother's lullaby.
"Hmm… what's love if it's not the silly things we do for each other?" I said, glancing sideways at him while walking.
Soon, we reached a brook hidden by bushes, flowers blooming, butterflies and dragonflies dancing in the sunlight

reflected on the water. Ahead stood a great banyan tree. We sat beneath its shade.

I was happy—truly happy. The love I had felt with my mother was pure, the bond of child and parent. Now, this was different: the bond of woman and man immersed in love that was blissful.

"So, what now?" he asked.

"So... what's life all about?"

"It's about doing the right thing, the good thing?" he answered, half-questioning.

I held his hand.

"Can I kiss you?" I asked. Inside me, waves rose and crashed against the shores of my heart, drawn to the gravity of his lips.

He smiled, giving me silent permission.

I leaned closer, breathing away from his arms. Our gazes locked like stars drawn into each other's gravity. Our eyes shone with the light of our stories and the love we carried.

A smile spread across my face as I moved toward his lips. Then, in that instant, just as we were about to kiss, we dissolved—breaking into a million particles, merging with nature.

Such was our short eclogue.

Chapter 27: I Am Everywhere.

After dissolving into nature, I began crossing over. Leaving the body with a feeling of love and goodness was extraordinary. I was traveling into the light—an endless, boundless light.

What might have happened at the haunted house? The shield of love would have been shattered by the dagger of rage. Tom would have been alerting his boss: *"Boss, the shield is broken. Alert! Alert!"* Aarav, lying unconscious on the floor, might have just awakened from his dream—a dream that felt like reality. Perhaps he may be humming his mother's lullaby.

His master, Rudranetra, might have stormed into the haunted house and scolded him: *"What were you thinking, child? Do you know how a human behaves when entrusted with full power? And you gave that power to a spirit? What were you thinking?"*

"But the spirit did nothing rogue. It was only crossing over," Aarav would have replied.

"But you took a risk. You created something that lasted only momentarily, yet it was dangerous for the world," his master would have said.

Aarav would have remained silent.

"You gave it ultimate power?" Rudranetra might have shouted.

"I only showed that everyone has the freedom to do anything, to become anything. That freedom must be used responsibly. The spirit used it wisely and crossed over. There is no danger anymore," Aarav would have explained, his patient tone clashing against his master's arrogance.

And then, they might have dispersed from the house.

As I travelled through the endless light, his final words—*freedom* and *responsibility*—echoed in my mind. *So am I free to become anything? Truly?* I pondered the question for a while.

Then I realized my consciousness still existed. Had I not crossed over yet? It had been some time now, drifting in the endless light. And since I had freedom, I decided to become something.

I became a star. I twinkled far away from Earth. Scientifically, my light would take a thousand years to reach the planet. It was an amazing feeling to be a star, but soon boredom crept in. I reminded myself to act responsibly—perhaps some Earth-like planets nearby were using my power.

Then came my death as a star, a supernova explosion. Another star would take my place. But I transformed into a black hole. I was dark—very dark. I pulled in everything that came near me with the force of my gravity. It was thrilling for a time, but my existence as a black hole also ended.

Then, I chose to be a cloud. Clouds belong to Earth, but still, I chose it. I became a wandering cloud drifting across the planet Earth. I traversed mountains, valleys, and vast oceans. Obstructing the sunlight over them was a play. And moving aside, and letting the sun rays light them up was a joy. I drifted and drifted until I reached the place where it all began—the haunted house on the hill.

Chapter 28: Electronic Impulses Continue.

The haunted house on the hill was still there. But it was no longer haunted. How could it be? I am no longer a ghost, right?

I drifted closer, into the troposphere, to take a clearer look. The house hadn't changed much. What? Thousands of years had passed, and yet the house remained almost the same? The thought intrigued me.

Perhaps the concept of time doesn't work the same everywhere in the universe. *"Have I lived thousands of years that are only a few minutes on this planet?"* I wondered.

My heart raced with curiosity thinking, "what if it was only five minutes on planet Earth." I inspected every part of the hill.

And there—yes, there—I found a man. Young, handsome, long hair, a kind face. He was still climbing down the hill with his bot. I could not believe myself that he was still their climbing down the hill.

I shifted from cloud to electronic impulses. The impulses surged forward and flew into circuitry of the talking bot the stranger carried. The bot sputtered, making strange sounds.

"Tom, what's happening?" the stranger asked, lines forming on his forehead.

"Boss, it's... argh..." Tom began to babble, but I cut him off and said, in my own voice, I said "Hey stranger!"

He wasn't shocked. He simply smiled, as if he had always known I would return. His smile told me he somehow understood my entire journey.

And behind him, the haunted house on the hill began to fade—bit by bit—until it disappeared completely.

So, what is the most beautiful thing I have encountered in life after my brave mother? It is this extraordinary human being, who holds all the powers of the universe yet chooses to be content with small acts of love and kindness.

I will gaze at him for eternity with the same awe and wonder I feel when looking at the stars in the night sky. I was made for that—for losing myself completely in the act of looking at him with love forever.

Afterword

This book is inspired by a thought that came after reading a depressing newspaper article which read *'A father kills his new born daughter in the hospital. He was angry over the baby being a girl.'*

What if the baby was saved by her mother – a mother who not only looked after her safety from the father but who also became a hero role model for the child by being strong and independent. With some difficulties, the daughter-mother duo may have a great time until they have to face a bigger problem called as 'Society'.

Some rules of the society from time immemorial are as follows. A girl should leave her parents. Princesses should move to Prince's kingdom post marriage. Queens should live in King's land post marriage. Wife should live with husband's family post marriage. There is very little scope for a daughter to contribute towards her own family.

The women are expected to take care of not only her husband but also her husband's family. They are also expected to bring wealth in the form of dowry (– dowry system which is fading?). She is expected to be polite with everyone in her new family regardless of how they treat her.

On top of that, a woman without a boy child is treated as inferior.

Sometimes, especially when the husband and his family is crooked, these women also have to suffer in silence. They have to bear with verbal, physical, and mental abuse. Sometimes, these abuses can take form of torture. Sometimes, torture can also lead to killings, though it is rare.

These strange rules of the society may have induced fear of girl child in her father's mind. Has this fear made him kill his daughter on her first day of life – a day which should have been celebrated for the springing of new life?

This book tries to discuss about these complex situations of women in a storified manner. It tries to explore about what is right? About what the people in their rational minds should have done?

Other parts of the book deal with supernatural elements which are only fantasy. These fantasy elements shed light on living an unregretful life by choosing to do what is right and what is good.

With widespread education, society's rules—especially those related to women—are slowly changing. Hope flows through the pages of this book to contribute to the ongoing movement toward an unbiased, gender-neutral society that acts with maturity and common sense.

Bharani Kumar Buyakar

Bharani Kumar Buyakar is a writer from Hyderabad, India. His first book, *Once Again Beautiful and Pure: A Tale of Strength and Redemption*, follows a father's journey recorded in his diary as he tries to mend his broken relationship with his grown-up son, who is facing his own personal struggles. The story explores themes such as forced marriage and its impact on family relationships, workplace humiliation, current political scenarios, and the stock market crisis.